Taken to Revatu

Xiveri Mates Book 10

Elizabeth Stephens

Contents

Glossary

Cera *(seh-rah)*
No in Revatu

Cocorangee *(Coh-coh-rhan-gee)*
Sentient, translucent-white beings with claws and hundreds of legs; they spin thick webs between the islands of Revatu

Deliha *(dell-ee-ha)*
One who is trained in the ways of Revatu; i.e. Apprentice of Revatu

Dulaha *(doo-la-ha)*
One who trains either kits or alien species in the ways of Revatu; i.e. Master of Revatu

The Hunger
Nutrient-rich magma that pours from the Mouth; highly dangerous to the creatures of Revatu as it can cause severe burns and even death

The Mainland
The largest island of this unnammed planet; characterized by a large volcano and the primary hunting and harvesting ground of the Revatu beings who live on a linked island known as Revatu

The Mouth
The largest volcano of the mainland

Nebiya *(neb-ee-ya)*
Why?

Rax *(rhacks)*
A common curse in Quadrant One

Reevi shoots *(ree-vee)*
Bamboo-like shoots that present a common building tool in Revatu and are used to make furniture, build homes, and whose insides can be spun into twine

Revatu *(Revv-ah-too)*
One of a very select few islands on this unnamed planet that the Hunger does not reach; as such, it is the primary home of the Revatu beings, orc-like land and tree-dwellers

Sesiva'a *(sess-ee-vah—ah)*
What? Often used for clarification

Sevva-sevva *(sevvah-sevvah)*
Water

Shenti *(shen-tee)*
Yes in Revatu

Shrevara'a *(shrev-ahr-ah—ah)*
Rally to determine a dulaha for a new deliha

Sohifa *(so-hee-fah)*
Farmer

Taga'ana *(ta-ga-an-na)*
Revatu oceanic beast, carnivorous

The Thirst
Rain that falls across all islands of this unnamed planet

To'ogo *(tow-oh-go)*
Ale of Revatu

Tre'or'oro *(treh-orr-orr-oh)*
Bonding gift presented from an interested male or female to their intended love interest as a way to seal a previously proposed union

Vevari *(veh-varr-ee)*
Trees on Revatu characterized by huge grey and green trunks and leaves in shades of purple, blue and green

To the stars.
May they always guide us home.

elizabeth

1

Grcyxz

I watch the space junk arc across Revatu's perfect green sky in great balls of blue fire. Beautiful. I set down the chrxzyt nut I've been separating from its fleshy outer shell and look across the small orchard at Bebetu and Orick. Orick's upper lip curls back even further, revealing the tips of his tusks. He slings his shearing blade over his shoulder. I stake mine into the ground — a challenge. I don't need a blade to best him and take whatever this haul of space junk brings in.

Bebetu sneers, her tusks jutting from her lower jaw to press into her upper lip — a miniature version of my own tusks, which are among the thickest and sharpest in our pride. The large flaps of her ears twitch in irritation, or perhaps anticipation.

I take off at a run, make it to the edge of Revatu before they do, and then jump off of the edge of the island.

2
Latanya

Rax! Rax, rax, rax. "Rax!" I shout the word out loud that's been repeating in my mind on an endless loop.

He's got me cornered. Rock and a hard place take on a new definition. Rocks aren't my problem.

Negunn is my problem.

The cliff behind me is my problem.

The frothing pink water below it is my problem.

And my biggest problem? This brown, gelatinous, raxing magma goo that's creeping slowly across the forest floor — somehow not disturbing the trees or the bushes at all, but meanwhile incinerating the remains of the wrecked pod I had to bash my way out of. The tracking device built into the hull that I had hoped to use is gone. I don't even know if my parents crashed onto this planet or another one, or if they made it anywhere at all.

Maybe, they're still lost in space.

What if they die there? What if I never find them? My heart seems to pound against all my organs at once, everything squeezing tight in terror as I look across the shrinking space between Negunn and me, hating him beyond any hatred I've ever felt toward him before.

And I've always hated him.

But right now, for all I know, the only beings on this planet might be me and Negunn and, even if we were literally the last two souls left on this planet, I'd still prefer the magma. I glance at it just as the last of the kintarr exterior of my pod's hull crackles spectacularly in a show of color and light, and then dies.

Alright, perhaps I prefer the fall.

I glance over my shoulder. There's only about a dozen steps between me and the cliff's edge. I glance at the trees towering above me, some leaning out over the steep, death-defying drop as if in defiance of gravity, completely unconcerned for the frothing pink waters below. Some of the branches and the thick vines hanging from them look close enough to touch... If I were to jump out over the water, I might be able to reach the one...

But I won't.

"Come on, Latanya. You know you never had a choice in this."

Maybe, I'll have to fight.

"That's not true." I ball my hands into fists and Negunn glances down at them.

He laughs. "We can do this the easy way or the hard way."

"What's the easy way? Because with you things have been hard our whole lives." I slam my fist down onto my thigh, which trembles in the aftermath of the crash. Maybe, the shock. Maybe I'm injured. I wouldn't know. My adrenaline is thrashing wildly through my body, making me hot, making me want him to attack. "I don't understand you! You're a Quadrant One prince. The females all think you're attractive. You're from one of the wealthiest lines in the Quadrant. You could have any female you want!"

His eyes narrow when I say that and his smile slips into something more menacing. A frown. "Not any female."

"You want me because I don't want you?"

"Why don't you want me?" He gestures to his chest, which is bare because it always is. He knows how he looks. He is the prodigal son of Quadrant One, every prince's perfect archetype. Gold skin that shimmers in the light, rainbow-colored hair that falls in perfect waves to his earlobes and never looks mussed no matter how many times he runs his fingers through it. Striated eyes that are turquoise and gold and pink. I've seen him naked before at the royal bath houses and he's got a gigantic cock and is perfectly fit. Muscular thighs. Manicured feet. He's rich. He's intelligent. On paper, there's no reason not to want him.

Except, I'd rather take the magma. Or jump for the trees.

"You're a creep!" The magma is casting heat. Fifty feet away and closing in from the left, it isn't moving fast, but if it gets within a stone's throw, I won't have any choice but to follow the path to the right — the one Negunn is blocking.

"You're just an adopted hybrid oud," he sneers the insult. It's a universal insult for hybrid bastards, the lowest of the low. It stings when he says it, even though he's said it before. My mom told me that words only have power if you let them, but I'm not sure that's true.

"Your mother is hideous and your father was outcast from the royal family for mating her. Their union is frowned upon by the universe. Even though he is your mother's Xiveri mate and her horns flake white for him, they couldn't reproduce. That's the only reason you're on Quadrant One at all. Because no one else in the entire galaxy wanted you besides two freaks that couldn't produce a kit of their own."

I grit my teeth, bored of this. Insults against my parents are insults I've heard before and I don't care for them. They used to bother me when I was younger, but my spine was tempered and steeled by the love of my parents — the two greatest beings in this universe, of that I'm sure — and I have no time for this. There's raxing magma coming!

I cock my head and wipe my hands off on my shift — the threadbare tunic all that's left after I shed my heavy golden outer dress. "And you ask why I don't want to be with you…"

"Come with me, consent to marry me, and I'll step off the path and make sure you get out of here and stay safe against whatever beasts inhabit this planet." He gestures to the magma with a flick of his elegant hands.

"I'd rather jump."

"Then do it! Because I'm not raxing moving unless it's with your consent and your hand." He licks his lips and brushes his hand through his hair. I can see the sweat beading on his forehead, which makes me realize that I'm also sweating.

"We're running out of time, Negunn…"

"You're running out of time. That raxing stuff will get to you a lot sooner than it'll get to me." He crosses his arms over his chest and I pray to the stars for a comet or asteroid or whatever it was that blew apart the Paradise Voyager — one of the largest and most elite intra-Quadrant cruise ships ever built — to come here and land on top of Negunn's perfect rainbow head. "So what'll it be, Latanya? Is death really preferable to a lifetime with me?"

From the first time he insulted my Lemoran mother when I was a child, to the first time he petitioned the Court to have my father stripped of his title, to the first time he ruined the reputation of another Quadrant One prince who made me an offer…my answer has always been the same.

Yeffa. A thousand times yeffa.

I look at the glittery grey branches covered in glittery green leaves jutting out from the edge of the cliff in defiance of gravity. Thick charcoal vines drip from their boughs towards the raging ocean below, which is frothing and snarling up at us like the mouths of diseased beasts. My resolve sets. My mother, if she saw me now, would scream. My father would kill me.

I don't answer him. I just turn and run towards the edge of the cliff as if my life depended on it…because it might.

I'm three paces away from the cliff's edge when I hear thrashing. I look over my shoulder and lose my footing. I looked too late.

Negunn's full weight slams into my side and he takes me down to the soft, dewy undergrowth. Leaves, twigs, and branches in assorted shades of glittery browns, blues, greys and greens crunch underneath our collective weight. He smells great, like some expensive cologne. It makes me want to vomit all over him.

His breath even smells clean, like he just chewed bray leaves, when he leans down and says against my cheek, "I knew I'd get you under me eventually." And I hate him for it.

I thrash in his grip as he tries to contain my wrists. "Negunn!"

Taking both of my wrists in one of his much larger hands, he hauls me upright. His gaze skims the length of my shift. I had it on underneath the ballgown I'd been wearing earlier — a ballgown that's now being repurposed as magma fodder. He meets my gaze and smiles from up close and I can't help it.

All this anger and rage and frustration at how he's wasting my raxing time when I should be going to try to find my parents and the other survivors bubbles up into my face and bleeds into my mouth and expels itself as a wad of spit. The slobber slaps him right on the chin and Negunn looks so taken aback by it, I laugh at his reaction.

He releases me, shoving me to the right, up the path he'd been blocking before. I think this might be my chance for escape but the moment I pivot, he grabs a swatch of my bright white hair and yanks me back. His other hand finds my cheek in the form of a fist. He hits me once in the face and a second time in the stomach.

Pain splinters through me, but I somehow manage to keep my feet and stagger away. Delirious, I continue. I hear Negunn come after me but he curses a moment later. I slip and fall against a large tree trunk. My heart is beating in my head and my stomach is throbbing in my toes.

I blink open swelling eyelids and turn around to see something rather curious. I grin. Knee-high, dark purple flowers are opening up on the ground, puckering as if in anticipation of the magma and then eating it. But what's more interesting is that these flowers are big and

Negunn stepped into the center of one and it doesn't seem to want to release him.

Good note.

He's pulling on his leg, trying to free it before the magma comes. I hope he can't. I stagger away. "Don't you dare leave me like this! I'm your mate!"

"Psycho!" I shout over my shoulder. I don't stop running.

I follow the edge of the cliff for so long, I lose feeling in my feet. The foliage is rough and scratchy and I've got cuts up my legs, up to my knees. The stinging in my stomach and face reduce to a dull throb and I continue cursing Negunn under my breath until the single enormous sun in the sky changes tint from orange to yellow to a pale blue as it descends towards the frothy pink horizon. There's ocean as far as my eyes can see.

A few crazily-shaped islands stud the skyline, disrupting the pink water. Each one is composed of pale tan rock jutting straight up out of the water. Green covers the tops of the plateaus, some of which are relatively flat, while others seem more mountainous, like the island I'm on that has hills whose crests only become visible when when I peek up through gaps in the canopy of trees.

At points, I think I hear Negunn calling my name, hunting for me through the jungle. At other times, I come across more of those glittery gobbling flowers. I avoid those. I have to double back at two terrifying points when I hit more streams of mahogany magma, and then a third time when the jungle just gets too dense to pass through, until I eventually break through a small clearing where a bunch of trees have fallen…and I see why.

"Mom! Dad!" I shout at the wreckage of a dozen pods. Maybe even more. Metal odds and bobs and kintarr crystals lie shattered all over the forest floor but, as I begin picking through the wreckage, it's clear that the site has been abandoned for a while. I wonder where they fled…and what drove them out…

I try to find signs that one of the pods might have belonged to my mom or my dad, but they're all identical shells. They look like corkscrews with a central hull in the center large enough for one person and some supplies.

Pain shoots up my left leg. "Rax," I hiss. I lift my left foot and see a huge shard of pale pink kintarr jutting out of the sole of my foot. Produced primarily on Lemora, kintarr is both beautiful and tough and is our primary source of power on Quadrant One. And it's expensive. Perhaps, the most expensive substance in the known Quadrants.

My dad used to trade in kintarr and the part of me that used to help him out in his business grieves to see so much of it wasted here on the forest floor, soon to be consumed by magma. It's only be a matter of time.

I glance around, wondering what produces the magma, but I seem to have stumbled into a kind of depression and I can't see much of anything through the dense canopy up above and its rich web of tree branches dripping in vines and hanging moss, like the gowns of Quandrant One princesses whose pretty parasoles shield against the sun.

I shiver even though it's hotter than an oven out here with the one great sun punching as big as a fist in the face of the sky. I waver on my one good foot. My swollen right eye and cheek twitch and a bout of dizziness falls over me like a veil. I reach out and catch myself on the outer hull of the nearest pod, but it's sharp and digs into my palm. Rax.

"Okay, okay… Rest. Regroup, Latanya."

I hunker down into the blown open side of one of the pods, careful not to cut myself getting in. The seat hovers above my head and safety straps dangle down around my shoulders as I take a seat. They've all been cut. Hm. Someone escaped from here. Hope. I start pushing at the panels to release supplies, groaning as I stretch my legs out in front of me. The glass cut in fairly deep. It'll be hard to walk on.

"Luckily, all of these pods have med packs." I bang my fist on the large drawer marked with a circle with two dots inside. It springs open and I grab the grafting wand and a roll of waterproof bandaging.

I shove a tube of nutrition supplement into my mouth and concentrate on sucking on the sweet-tasting block instead of on how badly my hands are shaking as I extract the shard of kintarr from my foot. Tears well in my eyes and drip down my cheeks as I do, but I brush them back, body filling with warm relief as soon as I get the grafting wand turned on.

Small orange light dances between the tip of the wand and the sole of my foot as the device mends the deep tissue. By the time I've finished, all that's left is a dull throb and a scab. Still not great to walk on, but it'll do.

"It'll do."

I take the grafting wand to my other cuts, though it won't do any good for my eye. Finished, I let the wand thunk down against the metal interior of the hull while my head thunks back against the wall. It's cramped in here, dark, too. And outside, the sounds of things are getting louder. If it were thing singular, I'd suspect it's Negunn and prepare for war, but there are many things outside now and Negunn, I know, travels alone. Must be animals.

I haven't seen any animals so far, which frightens me given how many things I can hear now. Maybe they only come out during the lunar. I shove another nutrition pack into the corner of my mouth and slurp from the hydration tube as I start to look for a light source and something to defend myself with.

I nudge a drawer open that should have contained a spare bodysuit and a pair of boots. The bodysuit's gone, but the boots were left behind and shrink around my foot until they're nice and snug. Outside, somethings thrash violently through the brush.

"Rax." I bite my bottom lip and poke through cabinets and cupboards faster. The thrashing gets louder, punctuated now by thwacks and growls. Many of them. Freeing a space blanket jammed in the back of the drawer, I drag it quickly over the top of the shell before hunkering down and renewing my search for a weapon. The weapons cache has been totally emptied. While it may mean bad news for me, it also means that there were survivors. I will find them. I am not dying here.

Heat more violent than the thrashing outside thrashes through my veins while strength and determination steel my arms. I yank an exposed beam off of the back of the chair above my head. It doesn't come easily and by the time I get the warped metal free, the thrashing sound is nearly on me. Clearly, the blanket is providing zero cover. I look up, waiting for an animal to pop its ugly maw through the opening — or worse, for Negunn to — while my body burns, ready…

Sort of.

While I hold the beam in a death grip, I wonder absently if the seat it was attached to helped whoever was in here survive — my mom, my dad, maybe? Hopefully? Maybe it was even Prince Algerathon or Prince Wegerawe, two princes I expected to get an offer from on Paradise Voyager before Negunn got in the way.

My mouth is dry. The thrashing is louder. Separating itself from the thrashing is the sound of...of steps. Footsteps. Oh rax. Negunn...he must have tracked me here. Raxing suns, the bastard just doesn't quit!

I pull my feet underneath my ass, ignore the throbbing in my left foot and my right eye, and scrunch up into as compact a ball as possible. Every single muscle in my body is poised to spring. My hands are numb around the metal beam. It's gold, except for the jagged edges, which are black and silver, like they were burned. But there's no blood in here. They survived. Just like I'm going to. Maybe. Definitely. Hopefully.

I bite my bottom lip just as the blanket tears free and a face appears and it — rax. Well, it isn't Negunn and he looks far too surprised to see me to be a beast.

"Ermmm..." The word is mine, not his, and he jerks back momentarily before huffing out violently between his teeth — well, not exactly teeth. Tusks. Thick ivory tusks jut up from his bottom jaw, so long the sharpened tips press into his upper lip, going so far as to nearly frame his nose. Even without them, he'd still look every bit the predator, with his black slashes for eyes and huge, hulking frame. Atop layers and layers of muscle, his skin is a mottled green, dark and light all mixed together. I wonder if he isn't some form of Egama giant hybrid because I've never seen any other species with that coloring — or quite so massive — before. Then again, I know for a fact this isn't an Egama-controlled planet. And I also know that no Egama giants have blood red claws…

Trying not to focus too hard on the serrated blades sticking out of his hands that already look like they've been dipped in my blood, I take inventory of the rest of him and decide where exactly I might best run him through. Built like a raxing tree with a network of roots, he looks a bit too solid and dense for my flimsy metal but, rax it. I'm going to try anyway, because there's not a doubt in my mind that this…this orc, creature, ogre thing is deadly and I did not crash land on this inhospitable planet, survive and escape Negunn only to get eaten like a roast by this thing and his friends!

I shoot up onto my feet, the top of my head rising only as high as his pecs, and with a loud grunt, I strike for his abdomen. I fall short when he reaches out and captures the edge of my beam, which doesn't so much as scratch him, and easily takes it away from me.

Well, rax.

3

Grcyxz

Bebetu, Orick and I are joined by four others. Not many of us spend our solars off of Revatu hunting the mainland. Only the strongest do. Only the fastest dare.

"This space junk holds life," Yrkar shouts from his position crouched in front of the shattered mass of metal and gems. We've seen these gems before. They're very valuable and burn for solars on end — spans. Already Slascax, Vevaxcra, and Nevo have begun gathering them.

"Held," I correct.

He agrees with a nod, withdrawing his weapon as we leave the others behind and continue checking the pods for life. Finding none, we continue through the jungle, finding two more clusters of pods. The second consists of only three pods.

"He did not survive," Bebetu says, frowning.

A fallen tree pins a pod beneath it, the trunks of the Vevari too porcine for the casing of this alien survival pod to do as it was meant to — survive. The being inside was male and was crushed to pieces beneath it. We utter a prayer to the Hunger that sustains us, knowing that it will come for him soon. We will need to collect all that we intend to before it comes, though we will not take everything. The Hunger demands its sacrifice. The Hunger must feed, too.

We move on.

The rumbling in the ground is subtle, but is still indication enough that the Hunger will soon come. We will need to be long gone by then. Back on Revatu.

"We don't have much time," Orick shouts as we pass into the final copse where over a dozen of these survival shells lie scattered. At first glance, there are no corpses, but we will need to move through the grove to know for sure.

I begin picking my way through the shells to find those with the most gems…when I hear something. A racket. I look up and see that Yrkar is already attuned to the sound and a low growl slips from between my tusks. It irritates me. I am the Alpha hunter.

I surge forward, moving ahead when he gets caught on an exposed mess of metal mesh. He growls when I reach the shattered shell first, though the sounds within it have stopped by now. I flex my hands, my claws protracting from the tips of my fingers, a dark and menacing red. Not many Revati can boast red claws and my cheek ticks with the desire to tear a predator apart with them. And there is no doubt that it is a predator. There are only predators on the mainland.

I wait for it to explode out of the wreckage and attack, but nothing happens for beats. And then longer moments. Frustrated, I begin to entertain an impossible notion, that the predator within has laid a trap…but the predators on the mainland are not higher life forms, they would not be capable of this. I have only moments before Yrkar frees himself and joins me and I want this kill all to myself.

I angle my body to the side and keep my right claws held high, ready to swipe down and impale anything that should attempt to escape or attack one of my hunters. With my left hand, I yank back the silver covering draped over the top of the broken pink and gold shell. I bare my tusks, flare my nostrils and clench in preparation to strike hard and fast...but my stroke falls short.

The thing inside the pod is a rich brown — a color so vibrant I can't help but think of the earth after the Hunger passes over it and leaves behind an oasis of rich minerals which glow in the light of Revatu's Twelve Sisters, her moons, and glitter in her sunlight. But the hair...her hair is astonishing. The color of the froth on our waves, it's bright white, utterly colorless. It falls straight down to her hips and even though there are a few tangles, it looks freshly brushed and well cared for. The creature looks well cared for, well fed, soft in so many wonderful, delicious places. Her breasts, her hips, around her waist...

My gaze is roaming freely, but I don't miss the subtle change in her body language and I know the moment her surprise at seeing me dissolves into the desire to defend herself from me. She shoots up onto her feet and is remarkably short for a two-legged being. She jams a piece of gold metal towards my stomach, but I grab it by its broken edge and take it away from her. I toss the weapon aside with one hand. With my other, I grab both of her wrists and secure them together.

She starts to struggle wildly, muttering what sound like curses, but not in a language I can identify. Her hair whirls around her face and I can't look away. I'm mesmerized.

I pull the thin, coarse rope from my belt and loop it around her wrists, then take the loose end and toss it up and over the lowest Vevari tree branch overhead. I yank on the loose end of the rope and her body rises into the air on a shriek. I lift her high enough that I can kick the entire pod out from under her, easily clearing her feet, before I lower her almost — but not all the way — back to the ground.

I lower her until she's at eye level and then I hold. I stare. She is...unusual looking. Her cheeks are round, her eyes are large and tilt up towards her hairline and they're covered by so many thick, beautiful white lashes. Our people don't have so many lashes and I find myself struck by the urge to touch her.

Everywhere.

Heat builds in the back of my throat and I choke with the effort of swallowing it down. Panic and a momentary rage assault me but both sensations are short and easily batted down. She is female, but there is no shortage of females. I am one of the oldest hunters, seasoned, capable of control. I will not fall into rut because of this one.

I close my eyes and ignore the sound of Yrkar cursing and Bebetu warning me that the Hunger has begun its descent from the Mouth. I open my eyes at a sudden pressure against my left pectoral. I see her biting her teeth together...she's in pain. She's cursing louder now and I look down. She kicks me but she winces the moment she does. I frown, hand snaking down and removing her left boot. It thunks to the ground and reveals a bandage and I frown, concerned that perhaps this female is not among an intelligent species if she is kicking me with an injury. How unfortunate.

I take her ankle carefully in my hand and examine her foot. I see no blood and it isn't swollen. Perhaps, the injury isn't as severe as I thought. Good. Carefully, I slide her boot back onto her foot and retract my claws long enough to lace them back up.

"Woah." Orick's voice is louder than I want it to be. He's right up on my left and he's staring at the female with his mouth ajar, his tusks on full display for the female. I snarl deep in my throat, the sound coming unbidden and involuntary. I don't want her looking at any male's tusks but mine. Mine. The thought reverberates, even as Orick whistles, "She looks like a gift."

An offering.

A sacrifice.

The heat rises up the back of my throat unrepentant, the first warning signs. I swallow harder and hack out, "We don't even know if she's an intelligent life form."

She babbles something then and, with the way she's looking at me, I have half a mind to think she's speaking in response to what I've just said.

"She looks pissed," Yrkar says, coming up on my other side now.

The burn in the back of my throat ignites and my tail slashes through the air, all three of its tentacles coming unbraided from one another in a sign of my displeasure. I don't know why I don't like Yrkar near her. Orick, either, but Yrkar in particular.

By now, the other contingent gathering the stones has caught up to us. One of them whistles high and loud. Nevo and Slascax round the female and appear on her other side. While I hold the rope, the others circle her now and I can sense her agitation fluttering through the air like the warning signs that the Hunger is drawing near.

"She's injured," Vevaxcra says.

"Her foot is neither bleeding nor swollen," I start, but Vevaxcra shakes her head.

"Not that. Her face. She looks like she ran into something face-first. Or she was hit."

The burn in my throat becomes too much to tamp. I open my mouth and feel it coming — desire... Cera. A desire to breathe fire. Xiveri. The word floats through my mind and I fight the impulse to slaughter everyone near her because she's mine. Mine. And someone struck her.

I can see it now, the swelling around her beautiful right eye and cheek. It seems to be swelling more the longer I stare, and consequently increases my desire to commit murder. The burn in my throat tastes like smoke and tamgram flowers. The purple and gluttonous things, they eat the Hunger with their wide gobbling mouths and so transform the soil, allowing the Hunger to travel through their roots and fertilize the dirt beneath. This is, in part, what makes it possible for so much life to grow on the rocky surfaces of our water planet.

In looking at her and in thinking of Vevari flowers, I'm forced to think about the ancient legends, those that spoke of the Mouth opening, bringing Hunger as it does, but on a fated solar when the sky turned crimson, the Hunger would bestow onto the lands a goddess and the goddess would bestow onto its Xiveri mate control over the skies. A legend though it may be, it has happened once before...

My heart beats firm and hard and my mouth waters and dries at the same time. It cannot be, can it? I am First

Hunter, but how can I possibly deserve such a gift? And more worrisome…how do I make her mine?

"Grcyxz." Slascax says my name, his brow furrowed. "You okay?"

Cera. I am not. "Who hit you?" I ask the female.

She's still staring at me but at my question, she says a word, one I don't understand. "Nee-gant." She says more and then shakes her wrist. Her shoulders are likely hurting and I don't want her to hurt.

"We need to leave."

"We can't bring her with us without knowing where she came from and whether her people…"

"She comes with us." I look across the space at Nevo and hope that my gaze brooks no argument.

It doesn't. Instead, she's staring at me in shock while Slascax whispers something in her ear. Like kits gossiping, the lot of them. "What?"

Vevaxcra juts her chin toward the female. The gesture is threatening. "This is dangerous. We should leave her here. If she survives the Hunger, then we'll know she can be assimilated."

"She comes."

"I won't allow it." Vevaxcra is a seasoned warrior, but if she thinks to deny me or defy me, then she will have to be dealt with in violence.

"You do not decide. The tribe decides." I reach for the female, slide a hand around her waist, touching the softest fabric I've ever felt. Her warmth beneath it is tantalizing. My claws retract immediately, worried about tearing her garment and her skin both. She makes a sound in the back of her throat as her body comes in contact with mine and it nearly sends me to oblivion.

Beside me Yrkar hisses, "I will carry her."

He steps forward and I slap my hand over his face and shove him back into the brambles. He falls and the entire hunting party goes quiet. All except for Slascax, the little miscreant. She laughs, "I cannot wait to see how the tribe reacts when they realize you want her for your deliha."

I snarl and loop one arm around the little goddess's thighs, just underneath the hem of that translucent white fabric. It is not a necessary gesture, but I want to feel her bare skin on my arm. My throat burns and the burn only gets hotter when I let go of the rope and her front half drops forward so that her body drapes over my shoulder. I can feel her bare breasts on my back and my hand snakes up the back of her leg — to pull her shift down, of course. Not simply to feel her…squeeze her.

I speak through clenched teeth as I glare around at my hunters. "I want her for nothing. We don't even know if she's sentient." It's a lie, one I can see reflected in the faces of these hunters around me. They know me better than they know the Hunger itself.

The ground is shaking more ardently now, the tremors running deep. Imperceptible if you don't know what you're feeling for, but we on Revatu learn this art as kits. It's a skill she doesn't have. And her skin is so soft. She won't survive out here.

"She can't be taken as a deliha if she's not fit to climb. She could be a risk for the entire tribe," Yrkar barks.

I want to bite his head off. Of course he's right, but there's no doubt in my mind that I would take that risk. There's something happening between us. Ironic, because I'm certain that I'm the only one between the two of us that feels it.

I notice she has stopped speaking and has stopped fighting. This concerns me. A female who won't fight can make no home here. Maybe, it's just the shock. If she has not encountered other species aside from her own before, this might be a surprise for her. I smooth my hand up and down the back of her thigh. Her ass is so close to my face, it's all I can do not to turn my head and take a bite. She smells so good. The burn returns with a thunderous violence, if it ever even left, only this time it's accompanied by something else.

A purr.

"Are you purring for the female?" Orick says, coming to a dead stop beside me.

"Cera," I hiss, though the purr in my chest only increases.

"He is," Slascax says with a giggle. She tosses her thick braid over her shoulder and waggles her eyebrows at me when I look at her. Her fangs are much smaller and thinner than mine, they barely peek out of her mouth. She and the female in my grip have roughly the same shape, though Slascax is much taller, more muscular, has a tri-pronged tail just like mine. She is, in every way that would be written, a much better fit for a male hunter like me.

But I've never wanted Slascax. I've never wanted anything like I want this creature…

This creature that may be an idiot.

Hmph.

I'm still glaring over Slascax as she stands with her hands on her hips in her tanned hide garments that cover her breasts and her sex when Vevaxcra says, "Do you hear that?" And a moment later a bolt of lightning stabs through my shoulder — the right one, the one not carrying her.

I drop the female to the ground between my legs and crouch to cover her while more lightning flashes horizontally through the air. "We're under attack!" Nevo roars.

"Too exposed. Seek cover!" I roar, grabbing the female and hurtling our bodies behind the thick trunk of a Vevari tree. Carefully, I peek out from around it, nearly getting my nose singed off in the process. "There's only one attacker," I shout.

The female in front of me says that word again. "Nee-gon." Her hand balls into a fist and I meet her gaze. It's full of fire. A little hate. Enough for me to know that this is a being with feeling and the ability to articulate.

I grab her by the outer arms and pull her closer to me while the lightning continues to fire. It is concentrated around this tree and I entertain two terrible thoughts, one right after the other.

"Nee-gon," I repeat, stroking my right hand down the left side of her cheek, which is now so badly enflamed its a wonder she can see out of her eye at all.

"Negunn," she corrects.

"Negunn. Negunn did this to you?"

She nods and smiles and very carefully, her lips form words — words of the Revatu language. "Negunn heveva-ana-akcata." Negunn did this to you.

She's repeating me.

My throat burns, only now, a spark has ignited in my chest. I'm teaching her Revati. "Negunn heveva-binta-akcata." Negunn did this to me. I point at her.

She points at herself and repeats after me carefully. I watch her mouth the entire time and when she's finished, I smile, lean forward and brush my lips over her forehead, my tusks, too. I lick a line from the center of her forehead to her hairline, marking her by scent for other males to understand that even though I'll leave her now, it isn't a free for all. This female has a male already. But right now, this male has to kill for her.

"I'll kill Negunn for you." I make a slicing motion across the neck.

Her eyes fill with pleasure. She grins ear to ear and the spark in my chest ticks again and again with the desire to ignite. "Kill Negunn! Kill Negunn!" She claps her hands together and bounces on the balls of her feet.

Her reaction surprises me. She's so soft and delicate in appearance. I didn't expect her to be a predatory being. When I bring her to my home, will she try to eat me in the lunar? The thought fills me with pride and longing — pride, at the thought of her fighting me. Longing, at the thought of punishing her for it.

"Okay, little monster," I tell her, massaging her neck. "Wait here. I will bring you his head."

I shout for the other hunters to assume attack formation. Once prepared, they release a series of coordinated battle cries that have the intended effect. They pull the attacker's attention around in a concise pattern, creating a lull in the lightning strikes that affords me my opportunity.

I scale the tree, find an ancient vine to support my weight and swing down from it. Lightning flares again, but too slow to catch me. I reach for vine after vine, moving in a zig-zag pattern as I advance on the creature. I can see the blast coming from inside of a dogo berry bush. I thump down onto the ground behind it, tear the bush out by the root…but the attacker I expect to find is absent. In his place, there is a single weapon, mounted to a gold triangle — a stand of some sort. It fires lightning at the sound of Nevo and Orick trilling, and then swivels left to fire at Yrkar's booming wail.

I swipe my claws across the neck of the stand and the weapon tumbles from its perch and hits the ground, dead. I frown.

And then a scream, "Negunn! Racks-ze-cowmehts!" It's a language I don't speak, but it's hers, so it too, feels mine. I look up and see the female — my female — running for the cliff separating the mainland from Revatu…but an ocean of frothy water and devouring creatures separate the two…and she's running like she'd rather meet that end than face the male chasing her…the male who set a trap for me, and that I fell into.

I take off running. The distance between the female and me is shrinking rapidly, but she's quicker than she has a right to be and she's too far ahead…I'm not fast enough. I can hear my hunters running at my back, but they are long lost. Yrkar is shouting orders to the others to corner the male, but I don't have time for him — this putrid Negunn — as it looks like my female is going to reach the edge of the mainland and jump for a vine…but she is not made for this terrain, she has no training, she doesn't even have a tail to help her balance and her muscles cannot be much…she appears so frail…

A garbled shout leaves my throat and, as her feet leave the edge of the island and her arms windmill through the air, I become certain of two things:

These creatures are capable of laying traps, which means that they are higher thinking.

And, this female was made for me.

Even though she has no training, her hands still manage to latch onto a vine. She swings too slowly to reach the next vine — the one hanging suspended from tracks of vines stretched between the two islands and that would deliver her to the next vine, which would deliver her to Revatu's safer shores. But it doesn't matter. She still took her First Leap.

She took her First Leap…

And I burn throughout for her. I release a roar that breaks something in my throat that was previously fixed. I feel unhinged, unleashed, and capable of slaughtering anything.

And I am certain that, by my claws, Negunn will die first.

4

Latanya

As I pendulum swing back towards bloody awful Negunn and the hot lava peeking in through the foliage behind him, I think about how stupid it was to fling my body off of a cliff in the hopes of catching a vine rigged up to another vine that stretches all the way across the waterway dozens of body-lengths below my dangling feet from the one big island to the slightly smaller-looking one. Because the thing about vines? If you don't grab onto the next one in time, you don't go forward. You go back.

Stretching my fingertips towards the next thick grey vine, I release a loud squawk — nob, I'm not even close. My arm muscles shake and I've got my whole trembling body wrapped tighter than tight around this stupid vine, praying to the raxing comets it doesn't break.

I swear I can feel his hand on the back of my shift as I swing towards the mainland, even though I know that's not possible. I'm still far enough away from it that I...

"Latanya!"

"Rax!" I slip, my sweat-slicked grip sliding down the vine about a body's length. I already wasn't so high up on the vine and when I look down, I see something terrifying — my feet, reaching the end of the vine and creatures in the white frothy waves below. "What the rax is that?" I scream as I try to pull myself up a little higher, only to slip a little more. "I don't wanna die here," I shriek, but my words are cut off with a loud, hard thwack.

That's the sound of my breath leaving my body. "Guhhh!" That's the sound of the half-gulp, half-shriek leaving my lungs as a huge weight slams into me and sends the vine — and me, clinging to it — swinging wildly through the air. I'm dead. I'm sure of it. I can already envision my body getting snatched up by the gaping maw of some otherworldly ocean creature, speared on one of its fangs probably, and that's only if I don't hit the rocks first.

But then…I register the weight and the heat that's suddenly surrounding me. Hm. Not dead. Definitely alive. No longer gripping the rope — the vine — with enough strength to actually hold up my own body, but I don't need to. I'm in a chair. Hm. That's not right.

"Place your hands like this, little monster." I jolt at the sound of his voice, gravelly and low and definitely accented by a language I've never heard before but one that's at least registered by my implanted translator.

His breath is warm against my ear and my bones tingle when his lips brush the side of my face. They're warm and smell like moss and the cold underbrush of the forest, the shade beneath the trees when the heat from the great gobbling sun is sweltering. Relief. He smells like relief. And relief billows against me like wind against a sail.

My body unclenches, muscles relaxing enough for me to be able to open my eyes. I look down and see my booted feet, dangling over so much empty space. And then I see other feet, two of them, both of which are larger and flatter than mine. There are only two toes — not toes, really, more like flat pads that are thick and calloused and don't have nails. He grips the vine between his strange toes just below my feet. Then he hoists his knees up so that they're cupping my bottom until I'm sitting fully on his lap. Tension bleeds out of me.

I try to look over my shoulder at him but am distracted at the feel of his hand on my wrist. He removes my left hand from the vine and I gasp as the bottom drops out of my stomach, but I'm still sitting there and he's still sitting there as if on a seat carved of the air itself, the vine swinging wildly beneath us while voices still shout from the cliff face, Negunn's among them.

He repositions my left hand about a foot's length under my right. Then something brushes my calf... something green. I jerk away from it, brain slow to piece together the fact that that thing is attached to his body. It's the same green color as the rest of his skin and I whimper when it divides at the tip, becoming three separate tentacles. They're thick, like giant fingers, and it creeps me the rax out how they move all together as one whole, yet independently...just like a hand.

I jerk away from them, but they dive forward faster than tentacle fingers should — in my limited, limited experience — and clamp down on my left leg. I resist, but they're stronger than tentacle fingers should be, too, and even though we fight, it's a battle I lose. He easily repositions my left leg so that it circles around the vine once, twice, and then around my ankle. Then the tentacles of his tail move my right leg so that I'm standing on my left ankle, the vine trapped between my boots.

"Now climb," he rumbles in my ear and he doesn't stop rumbling. His chest is making this most magical, magnetic of sounds, somewhere between a groan and a mewl. It's hypnotic and distracting. He must be reading my mind, because he chuffs in my ear, "If you do not move, I will punish you here."

Hm.

Hmmmmmm…

Heat floods me in ways it definitely shouldn't, especially because I don't know this…this creature, and up to now, I was barely convinced he was of higher intelligence! He could have just been a beastly predator for all I knew, what with the way he plucked me out of that wreckage. It wasn't until he offered to kill Negunn that I thought he might be worth a rax. And right now, I'm not sure if he's intending to be salacious or drive visions into my mind that definitely don't belong… He might be serious. That thought sobers me up.

His voice isn't pitched in a threat, per se, but I'm not willing to risk it. I step onto the vine with my right foot and push up with both my legs. To my shock, I inch upward along the vine. To my even greater shock, the male surrounding me moves with me at the same speed, but he doesn't use the nifty vine trick for his legs. He just moves up on arm and toe strength alone as if this is an every solar thing for him. No issue here at all. No frothy, foaming water. No creatures swimming inside of it, all fangs and claws.

Then again…

I glance at his hands, noting that there aren't claws there anymore, just neatly formed nails in a pale green color. I focus on them, moving one over the other slowly, and finally find his rhythm. His purring gets louder. "Good girl," he murmurs, the word coming through as a whispered translation and making me feel all the way down to my toes.

"My name is Latanya," I say, even though I know he can't understand me.

We were all equipped with translators on the cruise ship, since it was intra-Quadrant and the participants numbered in the thousands and featured delegates from all across the known Quadrants and beyond. Voraxians and Drakesh from Quadrant Four, buzzing, flying Walrey from Quadrant Five, brightly colored Oosa from Quadrant Eight. Even the aquatic Rounaii were on board with their scaled skin and single-fin mohawks, as well as a delegation of Ixik'tryl with their brightly colored plumage, intricate dress and dark purple beaks.

I caught a glimpse of a female cyborg bounty hunter who looked out for blood — a Sky assassin, perhaps, though I'd rather not know for sure. And I even had a chance to speak with a mixed delegation of grey-feathered Uonidian and the massive, insectoid Drek'Aljar of the same constellation.

Many of our Quadrant One princes were absolutely smitten by a female they were convinced had royal blood. She even had the same glittering gold skin many Quadrant One princes and princesses boast, but my mother thought she might have come from a faraway planet called Paladia...

My thoughts short. I catch a memory of my Lemoran mother, all regal as she was on the ship, even if she was one of the tallest beings there by half a horn. Where is she now? Where is my dad? Did they make it? The pods were empty. They made it. I'm sure.

And I'm going to find them.

…once I get off this raxing vine, for a start.

His thighs cup my ass and hips and thighs as I move slowly up the length of the vine. By the time we make it far enough up that I'm not in immediate danger of dropping off of it, he slips his hands over mine and nuzzles into the side of my face. He pushes my hair back with his nose and in my ear, he whispers, "Good little monster."

"It's Latanya," I say, body clenched — all of my body clenched…

"Ssslatania," he hisses sibilantly back. Beneath us, the vine has started to swing and, when I look up, I can see bodies in a blur as they dance through the air past us. One of them carries something attached to his hip… something gold. Someone gold. Raxing Negunn. At least they've got him bound and gagged. I grin at the sight of him.

"Ssslatania, is Negunn your mate?"

"Latanya," I say, twisting sideways on his lap so that we're chin-to-nose and, when he ducks his head, nose-to-nose, "and nob, Negunn is not my mate."

I speak in Lemoran, my maternal tongue, and I'm raxing frustrated that my translator works only one way. Everyone on the Paradise Voyager had a translator to understand everybody else, so there was no need to upgrade to the expensive model. Now, as the words filter through my mind, I make a quick mental adjustment to my translator so that I can hear my own words in their alien speak in my mind. Through the cluttered chaos, I come up with a word in his language — whatever it is. An important one.

"Cena. Negunn cena Latanya."

I release the rope to point at myself and he snaps, "Don't ever let go of the vines." He grabs my wrist roughly and fits my hand back to the vine, his fist trapping mine against the unusually textured rope. Kinda rubbery. Kinda hairy. Easy to hold onto.

I pout, speaking in Lemoran again. "You're holding me up, so I don't need to hold them."

He makes a face and I grimace at the confusing inundation of competing languages in my brain. I find a few in his and say, "You hold. I no hold." I point to my lap, brown covered by a filthy white rag, and his legs, green covered by a tan loincloth that...holy rax! Is that a bulge between us? My pointer finger is directed at the massive schlong tenting his covering, shooting up like the trunk of a raxing tree between us. Mouth ajar, my gaze travels slowly back up his muscular frame to touch his face.

He's smirking at me, lips pulled to the side, tusks poking out to dent his upper lip and everything. They're ivory. So very white. I want to poke one. His finger slides under my chin and he forces my gaze up, which is the most embarrassing thing ever since it means he's definitely just caught me staring at his mouth.

I bite my bottom lip, wishing I had fangs like that. They remind me of my mom's horns. I wish I had horns, too. Maybe, it's just the longing to find that I look something like anyone I've ever known. A longing to belong. A longing for a beast like him to be able to find me beautiful.

"Shenti, I will punish you, but I will not use that. Now, hold the vine, little monster."

"Latanya." My hands grip the rope. We start to swing harder, faster, wilder.

The wind on my face tastes like salt and sand. His skin smells like the magma that sloped down the valley, smokey and clean. "Latanya," he says to me. And then we're flying.

His hand lashes out and coils around the next vine. He grips it hard. "Hold with your left hand and release with your right."

I do as I'm told, though I'm shit scared as I do it. I curl my fingers around the next vine and feel a bit better when his larger hand covers mine. It feels more secure. I don't know why I get the feeling that he won't let me fall, but as he says, "Latanya," once again, for no reason at all, I'm sure of it.

"Latanya…" I point at myself and then I point at him. "Name," I say in my own native tongue, just so I can hear the way it sounds in his. "Gormavit?" I repeat in question.

He says a single word that sounds like it's a string of consonants with absolutely no vowels to bridge them. "Grizz," I repeat.

He throws his head back and laughs. His whole body shakes with the sound and I'm smiling, even though my gaze is hooked on his massive lower teeth. Fangs. They jut up out of his mouth, framing shorter square teeth in between. He shakes his head and says the word again. I hear it echoed by the members of his species that had hold of Negunn. They're standing on the edge of the cliff, surrounded by many more, all watching us.

Grizz doesn't seem to be in a hurry. "Grizz go?" I deploy my strategy again, saying the word out loud and waiting for the translator to kick in. It's going to take forever to learn their language like this, but forever is what I'll have.

The thought strikes with a surprising calm.

I can't go back to my old life.

None of us can.

Those are the rules established by leaders of the eight known Quadrants. Because if a planet is not yet known, as this one most certainly isn't, interplanetary contact cannot be facilitated or established. Not even for a rescue. Natural civilization building is too important for it to be disrupted because a bunch of rich delegates felt like having a party in outer space.

I still don't know how we crashed, what crashed into us, what we crashed into and how… It was supposed to be safe until the alarms sounded. It was supposed to be safe…until I ended up in the arms of a green creature with tusks the length of my longest finger and three times as thick around and…

And I'm kind of…okay with it.

Nerves wrack my body and I shudder up from the soles of my feet to the top of my scalp as the words settle over me like a blanket, once more. One final time. There is no going back.

I look at Grizz and see him watching me with a small, indulgent smile. A gale of wind strikes us and he pushes my hair out of my face, tucking it behind my ear. "Hold with your left hand and release with your right. I'm not going to hold you forever."

But when he pulls back on my hips and I feel his erection dig into my ass, I get the suspicion that he might.

I take hold of the new vine, but a roar from below makes me remember to be properly afraid. "What do I do with my feet?" I gesture at them.

He nods, understanding. "Watch me. I won't let you fall."

"You don't know me." I wait, then repeat in his tongue the best I can.

He grins rakishly and laughs once more and…and holy comets. Is there something glowing in the back of his throat? It looks like he's swallowed embers. My eyes are wide when he looks back at me.

"You're wrong," he says. He takes the vine and we swing onto the next vine, and then the next, and then the next. We've almost reached the far island when, against the raging of the wind, I swear I hear him whisper, "You have always been mine."

5

Latanya

Negunn and I kneel side-by-side in the center of a ring of orcs. There's a body's length of space separating us — a short body — and it's not enough. I also hate that we're being held together. Makes me feel like they view us the same even though *he* was the one who shot lasers at everybody. All I did was try to stab Grizz. That's not half so bad, right? I glance over at him. At least he's tied up. I snort and stick my tongue out at him.

He returns my stare with a confidence that rattles me. *What's he planning?* I'm unsettled. Like the hard press of an icy finger is traveling up my spine.

"We found this female alien when we were scavenging the fire stones from the safety shells that crashed on the mainland this solarbreak." The way she describes things we use on Quadrant One every solar makes me choke back a laugh and I'm smiling when I look up at the female pacing the center of the wide ring. Packed earth is beneath my knees, cleared of brush. A few felled trees ring the space and, just beyond them, I see the chopped stumps they once belonged to.

I can't see any buildings, though. I can't see much past the dense growth surrounding us. The trees are tall

— not anywhere near as tall as the werro trees of Voraxia, but certainly taller than any trees we have in Quadrant One. Nisinia, the planet my parents live on — *lived* on, I think with a heavy heart — is like most Quadrant One planets and covered in spectacular, but low-lying gardens.

And this planet, whatever it is, is hot. Really hot. I'm sweating. Am I sweating? No one else seems to be sweating. Negunn isn't sweating. I hate him for not sweating… Maybe, it's just nerves. Why do I feel like I'm on trial? I didn't do anything wrong. Except for try to stab Grizz and that would make sense to anyone. Anyone reasonable, at least. What if they're not reasonable? Negunn isn't…

"And the male?" One of the males asks the female in the center of the circle. He calls her a V name that I can't pronounce past the first syllable. "Vee, why is he tied up?" The male sits on one of the fallen logs, an axe stretched between his knees. It's huge. Half my size or bigger. Rax, this is a trial…but what's crime? And what's…oh rax…what's the sentence?

"He was seen chasing after the female. It's unclear what their connection is, whether they're mates, or she's his pet, or if he's some kind of predator and she, his prey."

"I am not a pet!" I shout at the top of my lungs.

Beside me, Negunn laughs. His head rolls on his neck and he looks at me with fire in his gaze. "You will be."

"Rax you, Negunn," I hiss.

"Hm. They cannot communicate."

"Cera, Mornar. They cannot."

"I can understand you," I shout, standing up on my feet, only to be shoved back onto the ground by the female called Nova or Nevo or something standing behind me. "I talked to Grizz!" I look around wildly, trying to find the male in question. I see him sitting opposite the ring from Mornar. He isn't looking at me. He's not looking at anything. He looks…bored, like he'd rather not be here.

I'm mad all over again. Here I was, thinking we had a connection. *What, because he shoved his boner in my butt crack? Get real. He's probably mated to a princess here.* I frown. "Rax you, Grizz!" I point at him and he jerks up, like he was asleep and I just stabbed him with the pointy end of a stick.

His thick, dark eyebrows furrow over his straight nose. He huffs out of one side of his mouth, lips fluttering around his tusk. He looks away…*dismissing* me. *What the rax is up?*

"Why is she gesturing to you?" The female on Mornar's right says. Her hand moves up to Mornar's shoulder and she rubs his back, the gesture automatic. Meanwhile, his hand leaves the handle of his axe long enough to give her knee a squeeze that tugs something forgotten loose in my heart and drags it into the light.

I stare at the female for so long that a stunning realization creeps up on me slower than the dawn. She isn't one of them. She's got black hair and purple skin and colored bumps above her eyes where I, and the other orcs, have short hairs. She's not from here. She's a *Voraxian*.

"Hey! Hey, you're Voraxian!" I shout to her in Meero.

The female flicks her gaze to me just as dismissively as Grizz had and shakes her head only once before she answers in whatever language is native to this place. "Cera. I am of Revatu." Rax. She looks pissed. Even

Negunn snorts at my side. Rax...I'm not winning any points here and even though I want to ask her a thousand questions, I keep my lips sealed.

Revatu. She's from here.

Now. It's like she's forgotten the stars where she was born. That will never happen to me, even if I'm forced to stay here for eternity. Never.

"I helped her cross the white waters," Grizz finally answers her with a shrug.

"But it should be noted that she made the First Leap herself." Another female speaks up and I remember her from the crash site. She was with Grizz then, and is seated near him now.

Her words cause a stir that brings Negunn's cruel laughter up short.

"Slksleiw, you saw this?"

The female called S-something — Sla, maybe? — nods. "Shenti. Grizz, Vee, Orick, Yrkar, Nevo and myself. We all did." Those are the names that I hear and that I fight to commit to memory, even though they're not really the names she says.

"Grizz?" Mornar asks, clearly seeking corroboration. He's rubbing his chin, the gesture either thoughtful or concerned.

Grizz, meanwhile, looks unfazed as ever. "She did. And she can communicate. She asked me to kill the male."

Another commotion. I don't understand if that's a good thing or a bad thing until I hear the Voraxian female laugh. A few others laugh with her.

Even Grizz grins as he leans back onto one hand. With his other he accepts a horn from a young, pretty female with little cute tusks. She smiles at him. He winks at her. I frown unexpectedly and I'm so distracted by them that I don't have time to stop the flapping of my mouth.

"I can communicate. I'm not a threat. I just want…" I don't know what I want. I guess, a place to stay? Permission to go back to the mainland and try to find my parents? A little help getting back over the vines? Maybe a suit that's magma-proof? "Water." I hear the word in my head and repeat, "Sevva-sevva."

More murmuring, this time more hushed. I stand up and turn around, wanting them all to look at me before they pass their judgement. Quietly, under my breath, I whisper the words I need to say. Out loud, I repeat them in whatever language it is that I'm speaking, "I am named Latanya. I want water."

More whispering. Finally, Sla stands up. She comes towards me, her many braids longer than my hair is and my hair goes all the way down to my butt. Like most of the others of her kind, she has dark brown hair. She also has a kind smile, a pretty face, and wide, black eyes.

"Here you go." She hands me a horn and I drink from it gratefully, finding the taste of the water refreshing and clean, if a little salty.

Meanwhile, Negunn says nothing.

"She is *not* dangerous and she *did* take the leap. We could bring her in," Sla says with a shrug and then with a grin, she adds, "She needs a *dulaha*, though. I nominate Grizz since she seems so fond of him already."

Dulaha doesn't translate. Well, it does, but I don't like the sound of it. It sounds like *master*. Nuh uh. No way.

For once, Negunn and I have the same thought.

While the crowd erupts in a very audible roar with many males strutting forward and declaring themselves suitable to be my master, Negunn jerks up onto his feet, his bindings keeping his hands secured behind his back and his feet secured together, but not enough for him not to stand tall. Almost as tall as one of these beings. And I've seen him fight with his stupid decorative swords. He's good, I'll give him that. And he's smart. Dangerously smart.

Frighteningly smart…

I'm terrified of Negunn.

"She cannot be claimed," he says and he shocks the shit out of me. He's *speaking* their tongue raxing fluently!

"How the rax did you get a two-way translator? The Eshmiri reavers didn't bring any in their last shipment!"

He grins down at me and it's wicked and I'm terrified. Far more afraid than I was sitting on Grizz's lap above the pink angry ocean. "She is already claimed. She is my mate. She ran from me because it's a courting ritual of our people. Many of the other Quadrants have such a Hunt. The Drakesh and the Voraxians of Nobu, for example." He gives the Voraxian female a small, honorable nod. "I would have caught her and then we would have consummated. But we were interrupted by your warriors."

I try to interrupt, but he just speaks louder and I'm too stunned to say much at all. "I am a warrior myself and I would gladly fight for my mate and prove myself in combat or, if you would take us both into your tribe, act as her…her *del…iha.*"

"Cera! Cera, cera, cera. Don't let him trick you!" I shoot up onto my feet and shove Negunn in the chest. With his feet bound, he goes down, fallen but not defeated.

"She doesn't seem to like you very much," the one Sla called Nevo says with a frown. In the pause that follows, the two females share an uncertain look between them.

"It is all part of the courting ritual," Negunn says in their language and I scream behind my teeth, exasperated.

"Negunn, I don't know how many times I have to tell you that I do not want to rut you…"

He cocks one pink eyebrow and says to me, "I don't see what that has to do with it."

I'm not *angry*, I'm frustrated, and for me, that's worse. I don't like stupid things. I don't like beating my head against a wall when I could be beating someone else's head against that same wall. I sweep my gaze around and it snags on the dagger on Nevo's belt. Decisions arise and fall. I rise and fall and when I come down, it's with that dagger trapped in my fist and a frustrated wail on my tongue and every intention of gutting Negunn right then and there.

But the bastard's good, I'll give him that.

He kicks the knife in my hand and it goes flying wild and then he kicks both of his feet into the center of my chest. "Puggh," comes the sound of me absorbing the pain and falling back over Nevo's feet.

She steps forward and strikes Negunn without another thought. "This is not some courting ritual," she mutters. To the crowd, she pitches her voice louder. "The male is not trustworthy. He shot at us with lightning. He has strong command of the alien weapons. He is dangerous.

"I say we throw him over the edge and let the beasts of the deep have at him. The female has taken the First Leap. She can stay. And if we find any others from the protection shells we give them the test and if they pass, they can be absorbed, and if not, then they'll fall to the beasts."

I do not like the sound of that at all, but I don't say anything because I'm more interested in the first part — getting Negunn tossed over the edge. I lay on the ground, in pain, clutching my chest, biting my bottom lip and praying to the great gobbling sun that illuminates this place.

"I have not been offered the opportunity to pass the test," Negunn says, voice louder than the rumbling from those seated. "I would like the same opportunity."

"He's right," the female beside Mornar says. She rises to stand and takes a step into the circle. I wonder if she's the leader…until Mornar, of all beings, disagrees with her.

"Geeri, I am not certain about this one…he carries an air of wickedness about him and his female certainly does not seem to be eager to go to him."

"If it is part of their courting ritual, should we not allow it to play out — of course, barring his inability to take the First Leap and pass the test?"

"I will pass the test."

"Rax you, Negunn!"

Mornar leans forward until he can grab hold of Geeri's pant leg. He tugs her back onto his lap, setting the axe aside. "But they are not on their home planet anymore and this is not an acceptable tradition here on Revatu."

"I agree."

"Aye."

Several more members of the congregation cry out their assent. Sla stands up. "Alright, let's vote. All who think the female has a right to stay based on the fact that she has passed the first test?" She raises her hand. The vote is unanimous. I don't feel relief. "All in favor of allowing the male the right to take the First Leap raise your hands."

I hold my breath as I watch several hands move into the air…then more than several…nearly half… then more than half. Only ten or so of those gathered don't have their hands up…Rax. I glance over at Negunn. He's smiling at me. I rub my chest, only to remember he just kicked me. It hurts. I frown, but I won't cry. I refuse. All I can do is hope that the pink ocean swallows him whole.

Nah, not whole.

In pieces.

"Then it's settled," Grizz says, taking a long draught from his horn. He sets it aside and wipes his mouth with the back of his hand like a slob. He isn't erect anymore… which I find tragic. He had an impressive sized…

"But I agree with Sla. He is a dangerous male with weapons he can use against us. He should be kept for observation. Let him work as a sahfifa for a moon turn. If he can prove himself trustworthy in this time, I will change my vote. If not, then go with Nevo's plan." He smirks, like he doesn't give a hoot about this or anyone. "We've already wasted too much time on this. There's much to be done before the rains."

That causes some chatter, most of it serving to frighten me. Why are huge monsters so scared of a little rain?

"Since we were not unanimous, who here is in favor of this new proposition? All in favor of having the male work as a sahfifa for a moon turn before reassessing?"

the Voraxian, Geeri, says. She lifts her hand. This time, the vote is unanimous.

Holy cow. If the princes and princesses of Quadrant One had to do everything unanimously, nothing would ever get done.

Grizz nods. "Good."

"And for any subsequent creatures we recover from the protective shells?" Geeri asks, crossing her arms over her chest and staring her partner down. He tries to kiss her and she evades, winning a laugh from the gathered crowd and a shaky, pained smile from me.

"We deal with it then. All in favor?" Mornar rubs his hand down his face, like he's exhausted, even after the vote reaches consensus.

He starts to rise and so do several others until a male who has not yet spoken says, "There is still the matter of the female's dulaha that should be settled." He's looking at me as he speaks.

My mouth runs dry. I look around the crowd, seeing only alien faces and multicolored eyes staring in on me. The females are mostly indifferent. The males look more agitated and I don't like that difference.

Negunn speaks without looking at me, his hands fists on his folded knees. "You thought *I* was the poor choice? Wait until you have to accept one of these raxing animals into your bed. You'll beg for me by the time they're through with you."

"Not even then, Negunn," I groan, rolling back onto my knees. "Not even then."

He sneers, muscles twitching with an urge to attack, but the female called Nevo steps between us and kicks Negunn in the center of his chest. "They're right.

Throwing you off Revatu is too good for you. You'll get a slow death."

Negunn pretends to ignore her, but I know he heard it, too. Her threats make me giddy with glee and eager to get to know her better. I stick my tongue out at him when her back is turned and when he doesn't smile back, I know I've won a small victory. Against Negunn, I never expect to win much of anything. Will never stop me from trying, though.

Meanwhile, the chatter has reached palpable levels with words being flung back and forth between increasingly agitated-looking orc-beings. The inhabitants of Revatu. Tusks jut out of proud jaws as males stand from their seats and step threateningly towards one another, making me worry that Negunn may get the last laugh after all. *If one of them plans to take me to his bed, I'm going to have to kill him.*

A female rises. "Alright, younglings, you know this isn't how this is done. Gather yourselves at the fall line. All those who wish to stand as this alien female's dulaha, take your places."

Bodies pour around me like river water around stones. Negunn is swept away in the opposite direction while two females — Nevo and Sla — pick me up by either arm and start carrying me back the way I came from, back through the trees towards the edge of the island where Grizz helped me swing over.

"Well, come on then," Nevo says, shaking her head. "This is an embarrassing Shrevara'a rally for a female with no tail."

"The males don't seem to mind the lack." Sla laughs, flipping her knotted hair over her shoulder. It falls to her low back beautifully, in ringlets everyplace it isn't fastened, braided and twisted together. It looks like a waterfall.

Both females have short tusks jutting up over their front lips. Their lips are just as full as the males' of their kind. Sla's lips are a slightly darker green than Nevo's are. Nevo is quite a bit taller and more muscular. They have on well-worn hides in shades of light tan covering their full chests and wide hips. Their shapes are very similar to mine, and it makes me think that we might have some shared ancestry.

"Vee, what do you think?" Sla calls out as we emerge from the trees and arrive close to the edge of the island they called Revatu.

I have a momentary panic that they're going to toss me over the cliff and dig my heels into the ground, but Sla and Nevo hardly seem to notice my efforts and just pick me up and keep going with a dismissive chuckle.

"Yrkar."

"Yrkar? Over Grizz?"

Vee tosses up a blade, catches it and slips it back into the slick black belt she wears around her hips. "Would have been Grizz, if he were participating." She shrugs, like that doesn't just grate my skin right off.

"What a jerk! Why wouldn't he want me for his dulaha?" I shout, drawing the females' attention to me.

They freeze, share a look, then laugh wildly. They say something together I don't manage to catch, not over the sound of the horn. It blares and some of the riotous chatter settles and I'm shoved to the front where I can see a line of male orcs standing with their toes pressed just to the edge of the soil…right at the edge of the cliff…

My stomach lurches up into my throat at the sight of them all just standing there, laughing between each other like the wind isn't eager to push them all off and into monster-infested waters. I want to close my eyes against the sight of it, but I'm distracted when a male starts speaking…and then is interrupted by Grizz, walking out of the crowd with his horn of water or ale or whatever it is in hand.

He tosses it over his shoulder and gives the other gathered males a wry smile, "I can't have it said that I'm not the fastest male of Revatu."

That wins him a few head shakes and laughs, some teasing sounds from the crowd. I frown. They're about to plummet to their deaths for comet's sake!

"What's happening?" I ask. I'm still being ignored, so I wait, listen to the translation, and then repeat it in Revatu, Revati? Whatever they call their language. "Vevara'ana shefa?"

They all look at me and laugh wildly again. "You need a dulaha." Vee shakes her head.

"Cera, Vee. Cera dulaha." I snap my fingers at her and shake off the grips of the other two.

"Vee?" She jerks back as if slapped.

I point at her chest. "Vee." Then I point at my nose. "Latanya."

"Lata'anya?" she repeats, nose scrunched, brow furrowed.

I shake my head. "Cera. Latanya."

"Slatanya," Sla says, while Nevo offers, "Latania."

I groan, palming my face, only to remember my bruise and hiss. When I look back up, the females aren't laughing anymore. Instead they're glancing between each other.

Sla says, "We should sneak him out and toss him to the taga ana." Nevo and Vee agree and lower their tones, they begin to whisper, but are drowned out by a second blaring of the horn.

"The final count for the Shrevara'a is fifty-seven!" A female cries. She whistles a moment later and several horns chime low, sounding like bells.

"Fifty-seven?" Nevo hisses over the top of my head to Sla. "Even Geeri didn't have so many."

Sla gives Nevo a look. "We all saw what happened when Geeri took a mate. Perhaps, the males want a chance to see if they can be the next Mornar..."

"It would be an insult for her dulaha to claim her for a mate," Vee cuts in. "Even Mornar knew better than to violate the bond between dulaha and deliha. He allowed another the honor of acting as her dulaha while he went about courting her the proper way."

"You know how foolish males can be." Sla rolls her eyes, a gesture that I find so eerily familiar it irks me.

Nevo nods, expression thoughtful. "And it *has* happened before. Not without rectification through the giving of tre'or'oro, of course — "

"*Or* without seeking forgiveness from the tribe." Vee nods. "Such a messy affair, none of these males *better* have designs on this female if they're stepping up to act as her dulaha. And if Grizz wishes to court her, he knows what needs to be done. He needs to seek her permission, she needs to decide on her tre'or'oro and he needs to provide it before another suitor does..."

"Why would he do that? He didn't seem to like her." Nevo frowns, glancing down at me — the first time any of the females has in several moments.

I frown right back at her, irked and a little bit... *wounded.* It's not that I think myself to be particularly beautiful, by any stretch of the imagination. I look strange on Quadrant One. I look strange here. But with her words, I suddenly feel *lied* to by the look I saw in his eye on the vine, a look that said he desired me. And not just any desire...not a desire for the exotic...but a real one.

Then again, I know nothing about him or these creatures. I'm probably wrong. The first time Negunn looked at me, I thought he wanted me, too, in a way that suggested I was respected by him, not just a thing to be used. It wouldn't be the first time I misinterpreted, or saw what I wanted to see. I frown as that *thing* that was tugged loose in my chest is buried again, an unearthed treasure chest covered again by sand without knowing what the contents even were. Maybe, I'll never know.

"Oh, he likes her," Sla says as her grin spreads slowly from one pointed ear to the other. "At least enough to vie for her as his deliha. It looks like he put his name in the running after all."

Nevo clacks her tongue against the back of her fangs, making a high, sharp sound. "You know Grizz. It would be an insult for him to stand down from this. He still fancies himself a prized hunter."

"Shh," Sla orders, crossing her arms over her chest, "it's starting."

They turn, almost in unison, each of them holding their arms crossed over their breasts. Sla and Vee have their chests covered in hides, while Nevo only has the one breast covered. The other is small and pert and dotted by a large dark green nipple shaped almost like a heart. When she catches me staring at it, I blush and turn forward to find that the large crowd swelling around us has fallen eerily silent, so quiet I can hear the creatures of this place — of Revatu — whirring and chirping and buzzing in their own coordinated cacophony.

Fresh, salty ocean air tickles my nose as the breeze rises up from the sea. My boots sink into the soft soil and, as I look down, I realize that these shoes look rather silly next to so many creatures with bare feet. My brown arms brush against their green — Nevo to my right, Sla to my left.

My hair flutters, white strands tangling with their brown, and my gaze strays across the line of males, nervous, but not so nervous as I feel like I should be. *Negunn isn't here.* I don't know what a dulaha is, or what the rax they were talking about regarding mates or the tre'or'oro — which, according to my translator, should be some kind of gift — but I'm grateful for that, at least.

That, and the shape of Grizz's butt. Round and taut, my gaze snags on it as he lowers into a crouch next to so many of the others, still managing to stand out…at least to me. *I want him to look back at me.* Maybe it's only the early wounds delivered by so many Quadrant One princes and princesses with their golden skin and silken rainbow curls that make me want him to look back over his shoulder and meet my gaze… He doesn't.

A horn blares long and deep and all of the males take flight. Cheers like thunder before a long rain light up the jungle. Sla and Vee and Nevo roar their applause, but I just gasp, because there aren't enough vines for all of the males to catch.

Half of them don't make it.

They fall.

They fall into angry pink waters.

They fall into angry pink waters filled with sea creatures eager to devour them. *Grizz could fall.* The thought fills me with an irrational and nonsensical terror and I scream bloody murder, body lurching forward like I'm going to somehow catch all of them, but Nevo slaps a palm over my mouth and Vee thrusts a fist up in the air.

"Seven qwis on Yrkar!" Her words cause a sensation. Bets slip and slide all over the place, but I ignore them all and stare, horrified, as bodies keep dropping like sacks of flour when, halfway across the divide, fights begin.

Mid-air, the male swinging closest to Grizz releases his vine, spins and kicks Grizz in the side. Grizz misses the vine he'd intended to grab and snatches another out from beneath a male who'd been reaching for it first. That male falls. Grizz keeps going, and so does the one in pursuit. He keeps moving faster than any of the other males and I notice with horror that they seem to be concentrating their efforts on chasing him and another two.

Three males swing onto Grizz, their claws latching onto his shoulders and back as he grabs hold of another vine, almost at the far side of the chasm now. He kicks them off, but they have him by the hair, by the trousers, by the belt at his waist...which he releases. The male clinging to him falls on a growl and behind me someone — Mornar, yeffa Mornar — laughs, even as the male disappears from view, lost forever.

My hands are folded over my open mouth. My hair whips around my face. I ignore it. My heart is beating in my temples and my toes are digging into the soles of my boots angrily. Grizz releases his next vine and starts to plummet under the weight of the ones holding him but, in a move I can't even begin to imagine replicating, he spins and kicks mid-raxing-swing, nailing the male on his hair right in the groin with his heel. The male tumbles off. The final male Grizz more elegantly evades, slipping free of his touch as if it were water when they both dance mid-air to the next vine. The male reaches, reaches, reaches, but Grizz, having already caught one vine, catches one extra and tosses it out of his attacker's way.

By the time Grizz has reached the other side and turned around to work his way back, there are only three other males in line with him and only a dozen still on the ropes at all. The female Vee mentioned earlier isn't one of them, but I do recognize another male, one who is leading the pack and was part of the contingent that found me earlier.

"Which do you prefer, Slatania?"

I jolt, look up and see Sla at my side. Her hands are on her hips and she's smiling at me with her dark green, feline eyes.

"Yrkar is younger and some would even call him the fastest male of Revatu. Grizz, on the other hand, is one of our senior hunters. He fancies himself the best. His knowledge and expertise would be useful for you."

"I'm sure I could figure it out on my own," I mumble.

She makes a face. "I know you can understand me, but why can only the horrible male you descended with speak?"

I huff and swipe my fingers across my scalp. Finding the stitching, I pull my hair away so she can see the three black pieces of what look like string threaded into my scalp. Negunn's would be silver — the updated model. "Translator better," I say out loud, then repeat the words in her language.

"But you can produce words in our tongue. They're awkward, but you can do it." She's not getting it.

"Learning," I tell her with a shrug in her own language, which sounds a lot like *vivi'iri*.

She nods once. "Good. Working at something is always better than having it handed to you."

I shrug, thinking about how convenient it is to be handed things. It reduces their value and makes it easier to use them for evil. Negunn always does.

She steps even closer to me, until the warmth of her skin brushes against me. She's warm, but not so warm as I am. Her breath is cool against my ear as she says, "Grizz is one of my oldest friends. You should choose him for your dulaha…unless you want him for your mate."

I feel my cheeks burn, though I know she can't see it with my coloring. I narrow my gaze and give her my best withering look. "I don't need a mate," I say and then, butchering the words in her language, "Don't need mate."

She just smiles down at me and lifts a brow. "Need and *want* are very different, Slatania. I don't care where you come from. You should know that."

Then she juts her chin back towards the swinging competitors and I look up in time to see Grizz and Yrkar neck-and-neck, swinging so far ahead of the others that I no longer bother paying the others any attention. I'm wholly concentrated on the two males as they release from vines, entire bodies arching like rainbows as they explode over the open air, covering unimaginable distance.

They don't bother fighting one another. Each of these males is focused solely on speed. I think Yrkar is faster.

He's leaner, lither. His tusks are shorter and so is his hair, which is also darker. Grizz's hair is a deep brown and reminds me of a forest under the lunar's light. The top half is tied back away from his face. Neither male is sweating, but I can hear their exertion in the sound of their grunts as they release their next vines and continue to swing…

Yrkar pulls just ahead and the crowd behind me roars. Sla just chuckles. "He won't lose," she says to me in response to a question I never asked.

"Grizz lose," I reply.

She gives me a funny look, then shakes her head. "Not when serving you is the prize."

"Serve dulaha?"

She smiles and then offers me an explanation of this term, *dulaha*, that makes me gape, but before I can struggle through a few more questions, she grabs me by the back of my shift and yanks me away from the edge of the cliff. We stumble back. The crowd surges forward. Yrkar pulls even farther ahead and just before he *would* have touched down onto the soil moments before Grizz, Grizz swings up beside him and kicks him hard in the ribs.

"Ooph!" The sound of his pain. Yrkar slides down the vine he's latched onto and Grizz swings right over his head.

Doof. The sound of the thud. Grizz thunks down hard onto the ground two paces directly in front of me, bare feet sinking half a hand's length deep into the soft soil — his hand, not mine.

Behind him, Yrkar clings to the vine, desperately trying to climb back up, but can't. His pained grimace is the last thing I see before he goes tumbling off of the vine into the water below amidst a roar of applause.

Now that this population of beings has reduced itself by a gleeful tenth, Grizz saunters forward, still without acknowledging me. Well, mostly. He gives me a quick sweep of his gaze and the stress of this very, very long solar must be getting to me because I hallucinate something quite improbable.

A slight glow that turns his dark brown eyes momentarily orange.

And then he smiles wryly and turns his attention back to the gathered crowd. He puffs out his chest, reminding me of Negunn. Only an ass like Negunn would strut about like that. He accepts the adulation and congratulations of his people proudly. They come to him and clasp his left forearm. Several of them press their right temple to his. It looks like a sign of respect, but I don't know for certain.

Groups of males and females move out of the crowd at a light jog. They form lines around huge coiled ropes, which they then fling off of the edge of the cliff. Everyone congregates around one of the four huge vines, each as thick as my calf. They turn their backs to the cliff edge and, at the coordinated call of one orc from each vine, they pull. They pull together, like they've done this a hundred times. A thousand. For generations. From their shared beginning.

The ropes rush and soon, I hear the sound of voices — *new* voices — coming from below. And then I *see* them, all the males — and the one female — who participated in this strange competition to be my master or maybe my servant — time will tell which — holding the rope under their armpits and *running* up the side of the cliff. They keep running until the ropes run out and everyone is back on flat ground.

Swarms of beings crowd around those who performed best while condolences are offered to those who fell early. Horns of ale are handed out — one is handed to me. A few of the ones who competed come by and talk to me — at me — offering me apologies for not winning me for their *deliha* and I don't know what to say, but I still *try* to speak. I get laughed at for my parsed pronunciation and awkward accent, but I don't care. I'm just…confused? *Nob, I'm relieved.*

I have no right to be but, as the lunar starts to approach and the jungle across the divide growls out a rumble, as if in warning of all its terrible beasts, I feel… good. I can't help but feel good. These beings are talking to me like I'm…okay. It makes me feel okay. And for some reason that I can't make sense of, I'm glad that my dulaha will be Grizz, even if I'm disappointed in what the females said before. *A dulaha can't be a mate.*

I don't need a mate. I need to practice those words. Maybe, on this planet, these beings will actually hear them. Because as I make confusing conversation and drink horn after horn after horn of the spicy, bubbly, absolutely delicious liquid that most certainly is getting me very, very drunk, I come to five lovely conclusions:

The first — these creatures are mostly good.

The second — learning their language is going to be a chore. It's all hisses and broken up syllables like to'ogo — their word for ale, or whatever this spicy alcoholic drink is that's so very delicious and making me so very giddy…I wonder, is there more? Oh shenti — their word for yeffa — good. There is.

"I'll take another," I tell the male that passes by with the large jug. He just looks at me funny until I thrust out my horn. "More." He laughs uproariously, so startlingly that I laugh, too.

The third — Grizz's ass *is* fantastic. I mean raxing stars, how did an ogre or an orc or whatever it is that he is get an ass like that? I want to bite it. And then I want to suck on his tail. It's fascinating the way his tail moves — all their tails, though I seem to concentrate on his the most. It reminds me of swimming, the way limbs look like they're moving through thick water, all slow-like. The tri-part unbraids and then rebraids itself seemingly at random. At some point he turns and takes both arms of a female in an awkward grip as they press their temples together, and he uses his tail to hold his horn. And I find it erotic.

The fourth — I'm too drunk to be leering like I am after a brute who ignores me. Maybe, it's Negunn. Maybe, he's ruined me. Maybe, I'll only ever be attracted to males from now on who don't give me *any* attention. Because, and this is my final realization, one that's significantly less blissful than the rest — Grizz might be my dulaha now, and I might be his deliha, but he still hasn't spoken to me once.

At dusk, volunteers gather up the heavy ropes and take them away, while others emerge from the forest with huge animal carcasses and throw them over the edge of the cliff. Just like that. Without ceremony.

I open my mouth to ask someone about it, only to realize that Sla and Vee and Nevo aren't there. In fact, almost everyone is walking off into the trees. A chill rushes up the backs of my arms along with the fear that I've been forgotten and drunken panic claws at my throat when I watch Mornar and Geeri climb together up a tree, grab two vines at the top and then just…swing away into the darkness of the forest.

"Hey!" I shout after them, stumbling over a tree root as I lurch to follow, but they're gone and there's no way I'll be able to catch up to them on foot. I turn around. Yrkar and his crew are making their way off to the left carrying those thick, heavy vines between them. More are leaving to the right. I turn a full circle and come to a stop.

Oh boy. There he is. Right there. Like he's positioned to block me from returning to the jungle. Like he might be here to push me off the edge of the cliff…

I swallow hard as I turn to fully face the trees and the male standing before them, arms crossed over his chest, horn clenched in one clawed hand, eyes flickering brown and orange like catching kindling. He's staring at me like he's angry…or something.

I take a step back, a root crunching loudly under my heel, which is odd. How'd it get so quiet? "Um…" I fidget, my fight-or-flight instinct telling me to raxing *fly*, even though I'm not sure where I'd go or, with the to'ogo and a sudden flare of heat coursing through my system in flares of unending energy, that my body really wants to.

Mmm. He is so very yummy. Is that weird to think? I decide I don't care at all.

My gaze travels up his body, from his two-toed feet to his calves, which are unusually long, to his thighs, which are unusually thick, to his narrow hips and his eleventy-million abs to his nipples, which are dark green and round as ancient coins. *I want to suck on one.* I want to scratch him. My stare drops to his claws as I want him, with a sudden ferocity, to scratch me.

Mmmmm. Yummy, indeed.

I get lost in the breadth of his shoulders, which stretch as wide as the sea and lead to a thick, veiny neck. He has muscles there, too, that support a hard jaw, which isn't straight so much as it's roughly cobbled together, like there's an extra bone in there somewhere, one that I don't have. His cheekbones are just as crudely shaped and make my lady bits sit up a little straighter in the hopes of being noticed by those cheekbones, by that wide, flat nose and by those overstuffed lips. Negunn has thin lips. Most Quadrant princes do... *I wonder what Grizz's lips can do...*

My breathing hitches and he senses it. I can tell he does, because he shifts half a step towards me, then freezes. I meet his stare. He stares right back and I my entire insides liquify into salty tears as a frightened part of me and another frighteningly sincere part of me decide in one fell swoop that I want him to look at me and find me not weird, but appealing — as appealing as I find him — and not because I'm *exotic*, but because he thinks I'm pretty. For real.

It's never happened before, not to me, and I don't know why I think it would happen here, when I'm the most alien thing he's ever seen. It can't happen...and I feel the loss across all my fingertips. I drop my horn of to'ogo to my side without draining it fully first and liquid splashes across my ankles and boots.

I feel it...but I don't break his stare.

His eyes widen just a little bit, but enough for me to notice, before turning molten. They remind me of the black lava. Black on the surface, but liquid fire underneath. And then he makes this jerky movement, reaches up and touches his chest, right over his heart, and has the audacity to look a little uncomfortable.

By the stars. This male who leered at me earlier and shoved his boner into my back and then ignored me all lunar long is looking at me like I'm the one making *him* uncomfortable. Meanwhile, I cannot begin to figure him out. What does he want?

"Well?" I shrug, breaking the silence with a swat of my hand. I toss my horn at his feet and he watches it land with clear confusion. "Sesiva'a?" I repeat the word I'm pretty sure means *what?*

He blinks and his expression transforms into an impish, carnivorous mask — one I've seen him wear before when he was condescending to all his fellow warriors. He's a cocky brute. I never liked cocky brutes.

I square my shoulders and narrow my gaze and hold my ground as he advances with that stupid Negunn-like smirk. He steps to the right, giving me a wide berth instead of charging straight towards me, and I can feel everywhere his gaze moves as he starts a lazy perusal of my body. He's hot, I'll give him that, but I thought Negunn was hot too the first time I met him when he looked at me just like that, so I know better than to fall for it. At least…I hope.

Then again, if he's like Negunn, all I have to do is wait. No one can hide who they are forever.

I feel uncomfortable. He's behind me now. I curl my fists into the sides of my shift, wanting to make sure it's pulled down and not fluttering up. My palms are sweaty. He comes to stand in front of me and is way closer than he was. I fight not to put distance between us but he must notice the way I lean back. Focused on my face, he raises his hand swiftly. I flinch and lift my left arm to block the blow, only to feel the gentlest trace of claws against my tender, enflamed cheek.

"How would you like him to die? Disemboweled? Strangled? Tossed over the edge for the taga'ana to feast on? Hm?" His voice is low. Too low. I shiver.

He moves around me again and my toes curl into the soles of my boots. I inhale lava and the clean ocean wind, the sweat on his skin, the flavor of his hair. Stepping around me, his claws move over my bare chest to the bruise Negunn left on my sternum. I pretend it doesn't hurt because I don't want Negunn to feel like he's had any effect on me. He's nothing.

"Disemboweled?" I answer tentatively, repeating the word he'd used.

He chuckles, his breath fanning the top of my head. Behind me now, his chest is right up against my spine, shoulders flanking mine. My toes are curled up so tight I worry about exploding right outta my boots. I need to take them off anyway.

My shift feels too thin suddenly. I don't have on a bra under it. My fiorina gown had one built in, but that fiorina, like everything else of value on Quadrant One, is long gone now. We can't go back. It isn't permitted. And a rescue mission is out of the question for a people with two thousand princes, a dozen of which they can afford to lose. I know that… I know that… I'm just…scared. Unseated and unsettled. He wants something from me and right now I'm scared, frightened by my own response to him, which is purely carnal and completely illogical and makes me want to forget that I have other priorities here. *Whatever he wants, my body wants to give it.*

He slides his hand over my low belly and my pussy lips raxing gasp. "With a knife," he whispers. I come alight as the pressure in my belly moves through me with all the force of the lava of this planet. "Or with my claws?" He drags his claws across my stomach in one gentle, yet threatening motion and I'm reminded just how easily he could do it.

"Claws." My mouth is dry. I nod. "Claws…"

He makes this purring sound deep in his throat and my entire body shivers with the force of it when he pulls me even closer. "Good. We will wait for him to make a mistake, and he will. When he does, I will do this for you."

"Nebiya?" I say. The word for *why.*

"Because I am your dulaha. I have won that right. And it is my job to serve you in all ways." He releases me and as he moves to stand in front of me, his mouth cocks up to one side. "Do you accept me for your dulaha?" He holds out both arms and I set my hands on top of his hands, which I can tell is not what I was supposed to do by the widening of his smile, but I don't care.

All I heard was his desire to serve me and all I can feel is my body's desire to be served. I've had enough of their spicy drink and a raxing horrible series of solars. Maybe, just getting over this strange urge and obsession — leaving my lust at the door — would improve my mood, and make me less uncertain about him…and all of this… as I enter this strange new world.

I nod, a little afraid, a little more confident. He's not asking to be my mate. In fact, according to Sla, Nevo and Vee, he *can't* become my mate if he's my dulaha. That thought relaxes me. Yeffa — or rather, *shenti* — maybe a good raxing is exactly what will clear my head of all things Grizz and help me focus.

"Shenti," I nod. "Serve," I repeat in his tongue and then, very carefully listening to the translations, I parse out, "Lie here together, Latanya and Grizz. One time only. Then find my parents."

He shakes his head, jaw jutting to the side in what I *think* might be a thoughtful expression.

I point at his chest and then at my chest…and then I point at his groin and reach for the hem of my shift. I start to lift…

A hiss slashes out of his mouth with such force, I jump. His eyes bug and his gaze drops to my thighs, but only for the briefest, tortured instant, before he twists his entire face to the side. "Are you offering your body to me?"

"Uhhhhmmmhhh…shenti?" My face burns with embarrassment, all of my confidence abruptly wearing off. What the rax was I thinking? I don't know anything about his culture. What if what I perceive as flirtation is just a part of it? He might not have any intentions towards me at all.

He opens his mouth and a wonderful sound comes out. It sounds like the mines beneath the mountains of Lemora, stirring to life. And when he opens his mouth I see something kind of funny. Just like in those Lemoran mines, it almost looks like there's a soft light shining out. Then the entire sensation cuts off when he snarls. His tail swats at the air viciously, sounding like a whip, and I jump again.

He starts to take a slow walk around me again and this time, I shiver because of it. *A threat. Definitely a threat.*

"Do you make this offer often to males who haven't yet given you tre'or'oro?"

"Tre'or'oro?"

"Their bonding gift."

Bonding gift? Why does that sound so ominous? "Cera," I answer, then carefully piecing together words in his tongue, I tell him, "No males give me tre'or'oro."

"You fear me, the tribe, your place among us. You want my protection." There's a question in his statement and I lift one shoulder in a noncommittal shrug.

He makes a clicking sound, one of disgust, and I frown, not liking that at all. Negunn would have accepted my offer. I don't understand his problem. "I am your dulaha. You are my deliha. As my deliha, you are under my protection. It is my duty to keep you safe until you're able to navigate the wiles of Revatu on your own so, in exchange for your body, you will receive nothing you do not already have."

I shrug again, wishing I had all the words I'd need to explain to him this funny, wretched, wonderful sensation that makes me want him and fear him at the same time, but I don't have the words. Not in any language. I shake my head.

The clicking sound he makes comes out louder. It's a little more than scary but I hold my ground because, somewhere along the way, I was wired wrong and even though my flight instinct is still shouting at me, with Grizz my natural instinct is to stand still instead and just wait.

"You make this offer to males who offer you nothing."

Incensed at his accusation, I round on him. "Shenti. Sex not bad."

His gaze forms twin daggers, aimed straight at mine, but they don't wound. They should, but they don't... Not like Negunn's do.

"Did you make this offer to N'gon?"

Fury lifts my arm. I throw it at him and hit him. Well, I try to hit him. He's, uhh, pretty tall and wicked fast and catches my wrist before my palm connects with his cheek. At the same time, his other hand snakes around the small of my back and he wrenches me up against him so that I feel every vein of his erection throbbing against my body, my soft stomach pleased to accommodate it.

I moan — I can't help myself — and his eyelashes flutter. The bloated mushroom head pulses between my lowest ribs. My throat dries, but I'm too mad to be appropriately appreciative.

My fingers form a fist and I yank down. He releases me, but with a momentary resistance. "Cera," I spit. "Disembowel Negunn, shenti?"

His breath fans my face as he exhales, his expression still sharp, discerning. "Shenti," he says. "How many males do females of your species take?"

Confused, I shake my head, but I still answer him in his tongue. "One."

"Good. Because males of my species do not share." He releases me, nearly pushing me away from him. I stumble and he catches my elbow and I swear I hear him mutter under his breath, "And I will not share you *ever*."

"Sesiva'a?"

"Come. Your training begins early. You need your rest."

"Wait!" I rush after him and, when he turns from me, grab his wrist. Heat flares between us and my inner thighs tremble. I let go and step back so quickly I have to windmill my arms to keep from falling. *Attractive, Latanya. Attractive...*

"Shenti, Latanya?"

Oh comets. The way my knees feel when he says my name... I shake my head. Not important, not important, not important. He said nob — *cera.* The moment's over. On to more important things... "I need to find my parents." I'm speaking quickly and I don't catch the words in Revatu. Revati? Revatian? I quickly repeat. "Find parents."

He turns to face me fully, slow in his approach, the embers gone from his gaze as the brown deepens to a near black. Concern. It warps his features. He reaches for me and I flinch, afraid, and that concern finds his lips, his perfect lips, and pulls them down. He touches me anyway, gripping the outside of my arm and rubbing it up and down. He pulls me closer and slides his other hand around the back of my neck, beneath the curtain of my hair. The gesture is so unexpected and intimate, I make no move to stop it. Comfort. He's comforting me. I don't...I don't think anyone's ever tried except for my parents.

"Your parents were in the survival shells that crashed here?"

I nod. "Shenti."

"And you believe them still alive?"

I know it in my hearts. I have two of them. They beat side by side. My parents have to be. "Shenti."

He looks into my eyes, each one, and I see my hand float between us. I touch the creases that have formed between his thick, black eyebrows. His skin is rough, like it's lightly pebbled. I gasp again and I don't know why. I can't help myself.

He clears his throat and when he opens his mouth, I see the glowing fire deep within him. He swallows it. "Then it is done. We will begin your training and we will find your parents on the coming solar."

"But…"

"You must sleep this lunar, Latanya. The mainland isn't safe in the lunar. It isn't ever safe, but especially now and especially for one who doesn't yet know how to climb. But I will teach you, I promise. We will find your parents. *I* will find them." His nostrils flare. He bites his lower lip between his tusks and I see fire in his throat. I want it to burn me all over. I believe him. I believe in him. It's terrifying. "Let me do this for you, Latanya."

I nod. "Shenti, Grizz."

He grins lopsidedly and, as he straightens up to his full height, he brushes his lips and his tusks across my forehead. "Come, Latanya. For now, let me show you home."

6

Grizz

Watching her move through my home among the trees puts me on edge. I stand in the entry room and close the panel in the floor behind me. I secure it by sliding a heavy piece of Vevari wood through slats that groan in surprise as I maneuver the crossbar through them. It hasn't been used in years. In fact, I haven't ever used it.

I worry she will feel trapped in here alone with me when really, I closed the door to keep others out. Revatu is not a particularly dangerous island but I feel nervous in ways I never have. *N'gon is much of the reason for this…* I grunt, hating that I worry for her and loathing that I worry about him. I could gut him in an honest battle without chipping a claw, but N'gon does not fight fair battles and it is clear he is willing to do *anything* to claim Latanya.

I tell myself that is why I did this so *badly. So dishonorably.* I shift uncomfortably as I watch her touch all of my things, laying claim to them in ways I'm not sure she's aware of. It humbles me. It makes me *feral.* It makes me want her to lay claim to everything in my home, me especially. Just as I want to lay claim to her.

I rub my face roughly, refusing to entertain such thoughts. I took her for my deliha. I had no right to do that and worse, I almost lost. Yrkar was faster than I was. Fewer champions fought him mid-flight than me, but that's no excuse. I knew I'd have more on my tail the moment I baited them, but I had to bait them because I couldn't think of one other reason to join the competition other than for the sake of competition itself. I didn't want to join the competition. *I did. I shouldn't have wanted to, but I did.*

Because now that I've won, I am meant to teach her, not to court her. And to touch her before courting her… I wince at the thought. The ultimate dishonor. *The ultimate pleasure.*

Because touching her is exactly what I want to do.

And she's offered to let me.

My heartbeat pulses in my cock and I growl audibly, willing it to behave. She flinches and the bowl under her fingertips rolls and the fruit perched on top of it spills across the table. She curses in her own tongue — it sounds like *"rackes"* and it must be a common word in her vocabulary because already I've heard her say it many times even though I haven't known her for very long. It makes me smile.

Her gaze drops to my tusks and her eyes widen and she flinches again, fruit spilling out of her grip and continuing a lazy roll to the edges of the table before dropping off and hitting the floor in a series of thunks.

"Sesiva'a?" she says as I prowl towards her. I pick up a large purple fruit from the floor and pierce the husk with my right tusk before peeling the tough skin back with my shorter, sharper teeth.

"Dogo berry," I tell her, offering her the fruit.

She takes it between her two hands. Her palms are a lighter brown than her skin. They're beautiful and covered in lines my palms don't have. I want to count them. I shouldn't have *rackesing* fought to be her dulaha.

I should have allowed some other hunter the privilege and I should have knelt before her and begged to begin courting her this very lunar. I should have brought her a fruit just like this and asked her to share it with me in the treetops where the moon shines bright. I should have asked her what she wants for her tre'or'oro the coming solar and by the coming lunar, I should have procured it and taken her to my bed as my mate. Okay, maybe that's moving a *little* fast, but still, how long would it have taken? Seven solars? Twenty?

Now, as her dulaha, I have to make sure she's adapted to life here on Revatu and absorbed into the tribe. I have to make sure she's capable of flying, getting around, traversing the divide and then, and only then, can I be released from my obligations as her dulaha and begin pursuing her as a mate.

It could take moon turns. Many of them.

Meanwhile, the last time this happened, Mornar was patient. He won Geeri in less than one moon turn and took over the obligations of her dulaha shortly after and by three moon turns, he took to the skies for the first time in his Hunger's true form.

He was patient in all ways I was impulsive. And now? Having her here? Watching her sink her fang-less teeth into the white flesh of the dogo berry? *Pure ecstasy. Pure torture.*

"Do you…enjoy it?" I say, fangs pressing so hard into my upper lip that I worry I'll break the skin. I try to relax my jaw and I succeed until she takes another bite and milky syrup drips down her wrist. Without hesitation, she sticks out her tongue — fleshy and pink and *ridged* up the center — and licks her dark skin clean.

I grunt, "It grows on the vines we use to cross the divide and make our way around the...islands." *Rackes*...

"Very taste good." She nods vigorously and takes another bite... "Tastes good," she corrects after mumbling words under her breath for a moment. I love watching her lips work.

Her mouth full, I place my hand on her shoulder and guide her gently to one of the seats at the dining table. Behind her, I shut the slatted window. On the table in front of her, I light the grey candles.

"Pretty," she says and I notice her murmur additional words under her breath. She seems to be learning from whatever translation device she has. Clever. Resourceful.

I smile and nod and focus on her face. "Pretty," I answer her, tucking her hair behind her ear.

"Shenti," she agrees, though it's clear by the way she continues to focus on her fruit that she has no idea what I mean. "Pretty table, too."

I nod. "Vevari wood. Most of the tall trees on Revatu are Vevari."

"Green."

I nod. "Vevari bark is grey, but the wood is green. I... polished it myself." She looks at me and I rap my knuckles on the wooden tabletop as I turn to face the cooking area. I pull the doors to the meat rack open and select several dried slices of modun, the most tender meat. I slide them onto a tray alongside two sliced modun eggs, horcu pudding, shree nuts and, from the cold tray built into the wall beside the meat rack, a dollop of whipped scre'ena, a sweet favored among the kits of Revatu.

I slide the tray across the table towards her and notice in shock that she's licked the dogo nut near clean. "Ooh. What this?" She grabs the edges of the tray and pulls it close.

I smirk. "Food. Eat."

"Thank you, Grizz."

"Thank me for nothing. It is my honor to serve you."

She offers me a small smile as she chews on a piece of modun and I wonder if she understands my words for what they are — truth — or if she believes me to be just another male in the universe that she comes from — one incapable of it. At least, that is what I am led to believe if N'gon is anything to go by.

I make a tray for myself, taking the toughest meats, hardest nuts and veiniest fruits so that I might save the rest for her, and pull up a seat across the table from her. Here, I begin pointing out the different foods and giving her names for them in our tongue, which she dutifully repeats until her jaw starts to slow and her eyelids start to slink shut.

I've finished my tray and am leaning back in my reevi-shoot seat, smiling at the sleeping, chewing female...until the last of the tension seeps out of her bones and she starts to sink to the left. I stand and make my way around the table in time to catch her before she falls. I unwrap her fist from around the last piece of modun, brush the crumbs off of her filthy shift and lift her into my arms.

My cock exalts. A grunt comes out of my mouth that tastes like smoke and spice and fire — a combination of flavors I've never tasted before. I swallow it down. If I transition because of a female who views me as an object of sexual satisfaction and nothing else, I don't know what will become of me. The only member of my tribe that I've seen transition with my own eyes is Mornar and he only transitioned moon turns *after* he and Geeri were already mated.

Nervously, I grip her around the thighs and back and, in this tenuous cradle-hold, I take her through my private reception room to my sleeping chamber. I've brought females here before, but this feels different. So very different.

I lay her down on the mat that's elevated from the floor by a reevi-shoot platform that I built myself. The mat, pillows and sheets I did not make, but so many other things in my home, I did. And she looks so *rackesing* lovely lying amid so many other treasured items, the greatest treasure among them.

A surge of…of *something* surges into my throat. I try to swallow, but end up burping loudly instead. She releases a small sigh and jolts automatically. Her eyelids peel apart with what looks like great effort as she tries to rouse herself.

"Shh…" I coo, smoothing her hair back from her face and sweeping my hands down the length of her legs to remove her boots. I'll need to determine a solution for her feet, which I realize are nearly as soft as the rest of her skin. A terrible thing. A *wondrous* thing… I knead the bottom of her foot, feeling its smooth curves, and she tilts her head back into the pillow beneath her and exhales audibly.

Her breaths deepen as I continue to press into her foot until, moving lower, her leg stiffens and she *moans*. The sound is heavenly. I press into her foot again in the same place, massaging it gently with my knuckles, winning moans from her on every breath. I don't stop. Because I can't stop. She is beautiful like this. And I'm a greedy, irreverent bastard and the sight of her weakened body rising, rising, rising towards pleasure is too pleasurable for me to give her what she needs — release. I mean sleep…of course.

I move her foot into my lap and take the other. The toes of her free foot flex towards my crotch and brush the bulge tenting my hides. The act seems inadvertent…until she does it again. A gasp flutters out of her mouth and on its wings, she whispers my name, "Grizz…" At least, how she pronounces it. And I *love* how she pronounces it.

A rough snarl rips out of me and I lurch up from the bed and move immediately to the wash room where I fill a bowl with water warmed by the device we received from the off-worlders. I debate, for a moment, because I don't want her to ask me about the water or how we warm it. If she discovers that there may be a way for her to leave… Cera. I will not entertain that.

My thoughts remind me again that my behavior towards this female is criminal. I have given very little thought to her own desires. I need to refocus. Calm myself. She's here now. With me. There are no other distractions or males between us. Her kin is missing. I will find them. I will help her navigate Revatu and, for now, that will be enough.

Returning to the bed, I clean her with a soft cloth. I dip it in water and watch it become murky as I stroke it efficiently over her skin. She sleeps soundly as I work and I debate whether or not to leave her covered, but only for a moment. Her shift *is* filthy, after all…

I remove it with a single swipe of one claw, straight down the middle. I sweep her body with my gaze, absorbing it with as clinical a detachment as possible. I can feel my heartbeat between my thighs, but I shove the sensation back as I move the cloth over her chest, under her arms, around her sides and down her center...over her core...which is shielded by a spray of black curls. *I can't have that now, can I?*

Gently, I ease my hands beneath her thighs, careful to control my claws which are eager to protract, and spread them apart. I bring my cloth against skin so soft, I worry even the cloth will abrade it. But it doesn't. The deep brown remains unblemished. One of the few parts of her that is. She has cuts along her shins and forearms and the bruising on her face and chest has yet to fade.

Thoughts of N'gon have no place here, but I remind myself of the oaths I made her. Before we are mated, before I take her in the way I've envisioned — in all the ways — I will fulfill them.

Retrieve her kin.

And disembowel N'gon.

The wait will be torture but, as I move my cloth between her thighs and watch her hips shift in small pulses, I know it will be worth it. She seeks pleasure and I will be the one to deliver it. The only one. Forever.

Rackes... Her lips are dark brown but between them... I press my thumb and forefinger into the plump skin on either side of her sex and gently, carefully, I spread her open to my gaze, only to be shocked. She's pink at her center. *Fascinating.*

"Grizz," she says, voice hushed.

"Sleep," I command.

She sighs, obeying quickly, the good little female that she is. *Such a good female.*

I clean her everywhere. *Everywhere.* Her ears, her breasts, behind her knees, between each finger, the crease of her firm ass. I want to sink my fangs into those plump, firm mounds and I'm so wired and agitated by the need that, by the time I finish cleaning her skin, I know there isn't a chance I'll get any sleep.

So, I pull out a needle and thread and I get to work.

7

Latanya

"Grizz," I say in mock admonishment as I glance down at my body.

He stands in the doorway to his bedroom with his arms crossed over his ripped, smoking hot chest — a very *naked* chest — without an ounce of guilt in his stare. "You're late," he replies.

We've done this four solars in a row and it makes me wet every time. *Every. single. time.* The first morning I woke up surprisingly clean and fully clothed, I was a little freaked out. And then that lunar, after a full solar's work touring the village learning the differences between the different types of vines and learning a few more words in their language, I passed out...but not fully...

I was still awake enough to feel his large, strong hands undress me, wipe me down with a warm towel and then fiddle with each of my limbs. I didn't understand what he was doing until the next morning when I found myself outfitted in an entirely new ensemble — he was taking my measurements.

Everything about the whole thing was so raxing hot. Him touching me where only five other males have ever

touched me before, in a way that was clinical almost…
almost. The deep way he rumbled when I inadvertently
moaned or spread my legs a little farther apart,
encouraging him on…though he never rose to the act.
And then finally, the fact that he's dressing me at all.
With his own two giant hands! No one has ever made
me anything before. At least, not with such care. Not to
care for me. Not like that.

I stare down at the funny folded hides crisscrossing
over my chest. They hold my breasts down pretty well,
but leave my stomach almost fully exposed, which I
don't like so much. My stomach is all soft folds where
everyone here on Revatu is hard edges. I glance up at his
face, wondering if he doesn't like the way I look when I
sit slouched. I sit up straighter. His gaze punches me in
the face like a fist and I tense, drop back onto my elbows
and spread my legs for him…

"Latanya," he hisses. "Get up. You're late."

I don't get it. I don't want to dance this dance we've
been dancing for the past four solars. I don't even like
dancing, anyway. It's too chaotic. At least, the way we do
it on Quadrant One. Though I must say, dancing on
Lemora is a lot more fun, depending on the clan and the
tavern.

I think back on the first patchwork conversation on
sex Grizz and I had and how horrified he'd been by my
admission that I didn't get presents from males before
sleeping with them. Then, I roll my eyes, disappointed in
him. And I hold onto that disappointment as I roll onto
my side.

Quadrant One is a sexually free place — there, *I'm* the
prude. Here it seems, I might as well be a sexual deviant,
even though I'm only trying to work this horrible,

magnificent friction between us out of my system. It's too distracting. And I can't afford to be distracted.

"Are we going to the mainland this solar?" I huff as I untangle my limbs from the sheets and rise wobbly onto my feet. This is a sentence I've managed to perfect as I've asked it every solar. Multiple times. All solar long… That's how I already know his answer.

"Cera. You cannot cross the divide."

"You…help me," I say with the help of my translator.

"Too dangerous." He clicks his tongue against the back of his tusks. His tongue is charcoal grey and looks rough and lizard-like. I want to suck on it. I want to feel it between my legs.

"Four solars too long," I stutter out, still having to rely on the words spoken through my translator and repeated in order to make myself understood.

"Your people escaped the pods. So did you. There is no reason to believe that they aren't still alive. And my team has been searching."

Every solar after our lessons he's left me behind with either Sla, Nevo or Vee and led a team of hunters to the mainland to try to find my parents. At least, that's what he alleges he's doing. I'm starting to doubt him, though. I mean, he hasn't found *anything?* Not one shred of evidence of their survival? If his numbers are right, then forty open pods have been discovered, each one containing one being. That's too many not to make a mark on the soil at all.

I step up close to him and narrow my gaze. Behind clenched teeth, I hiss, "You *want* me. You must give tre'or'oro first. Why not try harder for tre'or'oro? Why not try harder for parents?"

His hand moves faster than I've seen it outside of when he swings from vine to vine. He grabs the back of my neck and wrenches my face up to his, pulling me onto the tips of my toes. My heart jumps into my throat, along with a healthy helping of fear, but I hold my ground even as he growls, "Parents are *not* tre'or'oro. Your family can never be given or taken away from you. Your family is owed to you as a member of this tribe and I will bring them to you. After, you may tell me what you'd like for tre'or'oro and after and only after I deliver it may we…join…"

"Rax your rules. Rules, rules, far too many rules! Vines, then words, then…" I stammer, not knowing how to say what I want to say and not having the patience for it. I grab his hand on the back of my head and rip his fingers away. He lets me.

I rock back onto my heels and gesture wildly between us. "Cera understand this. But four solars is too many solars. I want…see. I want look. My parents *mine*. Not you. You…not family."

The orange flame swirling through his brown irises ignites then, turning his eyes bright red. It starts to bleed out of his irises too, swarming like stinging insects from Quadrant One, threatening to blot out his pupils. I know I should be scared, but my rage is momentarily piqued. He reaches for my face, but I jerk out from his grip.

A cramp picks up in my gut the moment I do that has me wanting to double over, but I know it's probably just my moon blood threatening its early arrival and ignore it. I spin on my heel, turning my back on him. I pass through the next room, which has some woven and wooden seating and huge skylights overhead that, right now, are uncovered. It's beautiful in here, but I ignore that, too, and head into the next room, which has the eating table and two trays already decked out lying on top of it.

I ignore the gesture and eat mechanically, a sinking feeling in my stomach that only gets worse as he sits down in his usual seat across from me. I ignore him, finish up quickly and clean my tray, knowing now which drawers to put the refuse in and where to take the refuse after. They recycle everything on Revatu. Meanwhile, on Quadrant One, we just shoot all of our waste off into space. I tend to think this way's a bit…I don't know… better?

I take Grizz's tray away from him before he's fully finished eating, just to be petty, which only makes me feel vindictive rather than vindicated. I'm frowning by the time Grizz throws open the locked port hole and releases the vine. And I'm frazzled, face hot, stomach pooling with cramps and heat as I slide down it to the soft soil below and make my way toward the village.

A female called Pri-something meets Grizz and me in the convening square where she guides me to Revatu's version of a greenhouse. As she gives me a tour of various dangerous plants I might encounter on the mainland, I realize that Grizz is *frowning*. His lips are peeled back and his tusks are almost fully exposed and manage to look terribly menacing. *Comets, it's so hot.*

I squeeze my knees together, knowing that his distraction is going to hold me back from mastering this and earning enough confidence from Grizz that he'll take me to the mainland, but I…can't stop. I'm totally unable to look away from him. It's like he has his own gravitational pull, but somehow I'm the only one affected by it. In fact, I'm not even sure Pri has paid

Grizz any attention until I get the answers wrong three out of four times when Pri quizzes me.

She clears her throat. "Grizz." And then again more forcefully when he doesn't so much as flinch, but just continues staring down at the last plant she explained — a large green flower with orange and green tentacles growing out of its center. A healing shrub, I think she said, though maybe I'm confusing it with the orange flower that has blue tentacles that'll kill you if its ink gets on your skin. Hm. I should probably know the difference. Instead, I'm only proving Grizz's point. I'm not ready for the mainland, but I wasn't ready to crash land on an alien planet, either, and so far, I'm handling that just fine.

Well, I'm handling it okay.

Because right now, my biggest ally is glaring around at everything like he hates it — me, in particular.

"Grizz?" Pri says again.

He startles on a growl, his shoulders seizing up by his ears. He glances between Pri and me, tense as ever as his gaze settles on me and rests there like a raxing boulder on my leg, like he fully expects me to gnaw my way free. I square up in retaliation, shoulder blades pulling together, chin tucking down into my neck, fists squeezing, *pussy clenching…*

And then Pri steps between us. "Grizz, I think Yrkar wants to ask you about something." She gestures towards the greenhouse's only exit, a large, hide flap-covered opening in one wall. The roof arches over our heads, made of the same shoots tied together that most of the furniture is. I think she told me the name of it already, but I can't remember what it's called.

Grizz turns his glare to Pri — I can see his lethal expression over Pri's shoulder, but she isn't backing down either. Instead, she gestures again towards the exit using the flower in her hand.

"Don't rile me, Grizz," she threatens, taking a step forward and wielding the green flower like a weapon.

He snarls again, but his gaze is successfully ensnared by the flower. He tracks it everywhere it moves to the point that even I edge back, away from it. *Ah. So, it's the poisonous one, then.* He walks backwards towards the door, passing long stretches of plant-covered tables. The tables are green, from the Vevari tree, Grizz told me my first solar, or maybe my second. I hadn't cared about that, though. I just thought it was incredible that he made it himself.

"Latanya," he barks as he finally reaches the doorway. "Find me in the training course after."

"Fine," I call back.

He just snarls and disappears, taking the tension… and something else quite precious to me…with him.

"So, you two are getting along then?" Pri teases as she turns back to face me, the tentacles blooming out of the center of the plant writhing dangerously close to her face.

I sneer at her, holding up my hands and edging away, "I hate him."

"Oh, I highly doubt that." She flashes me a grin with two little twin tusks that make me deeply envious, and then she goes back to her plants.

The sky is dark by the time I'm finished with my lesson — and not because it's late in the solar, but because the clouds have rolled in and the rains have begun. Cera, not the rains, the *Thirst*, as they call it.

The Thirst doesn't stop anyone from continuing to work, or climb, or fly through the treetops, but it does make the world a shade or two dimmer. A shade or ten. I found it a little bit frightening the first time the clouds rolled through, but Grizz had been there and explained to me that for as much as the plants and soil of Revatu and its mainland enjoy the Hunger, they enjoy the Thirst even more.

My wet hair clings to my neck as I pass through the central convening square, where my and Negunn's fates were decided. And, speaking of the wretch…I see him now sauntering my way carrying a stack of shoots — unbleached reevi shoots, as Pri reminded me. They grow like weeds, which makes them a common and useful building material. The soft fibers inside can be woven into twine. I know that Negunn's been working with the harvesters as part of his duties, but I don't know why he's walking towards me now.

I try to pivot. He anticipates and swings the shoots propped up on his shoulder to the left, barring my path, then moves to intercept me. "You're doing *well*, I see." He overannunciates the word in a way I don't like but don't understand, either.

"Shenti," I tell him in Revatu, refusing to speak to him in the language of Quadrant One. "Quite well. I can see you're doing *well*, too." I offer him a brittle smile.

Negunn's eyes flash down to my chest, making my shoulders instinctively curl. He snorts, "Has he broken you in yet?"

I jerk to move past him, but he maneuvers the stalks in a way that enables him to hold onto them with just one hand. With his other, he grabs my arm. Hard. "Negunn…"

"Don't tell me you've let him rax you, you little slut."

"Not without trying on my part."

His brow furrows and then slowly, creepily, relaxes. He lets go of my arm. I try to move past him again, regretting whatever I just said to make him smile like that, but he swings his sticks further into my path. "He prefers the beasts, then."

"They're not beasts…"

"They are. But I guess, to him, they're not so ugly as you. You know I'm the only male that will ever want you here."

"Do you need something?" I shout, frustrated that I can see other Revatu watching Negunn and I, but that they likely have no idea the kinds of cruel things he's saying about them — *and me, too.* The Thirst masks all.

He timed this perfectly, though I can't exactly give him credit for bringing the rains. Then again, maybe they bow to his will, too. Grizz has yet to make good on his promises to disembowel Negunn. Then again, why would he? Maybe, *I'm* beastly to *him.*

I hate Negunn. I've been feeling good mostly — less alien, at least, than I have a right to — and, with a few words, the wound that I thought was a scar is brutally ripped open. His next words lance even deeper as he says, "Your beast found your parents yet?"

"Rax off…" I push past him, ducking under the shoots and maneuvering swiftly, in a way that surprises even me, as I do. *Hm. Maybe, I am learning something in all my treetop training.*

He shouts after me, "Cera? That's too bad. Latanya, because I might have an idea where they are."

I freeze. Freeze and shiver. I look slowly over my shoulder to see Negunn smiling at me. There's wickedness and intrigue in his gaze. He's up to something. Or maybe, he *knows* something.

"How's that? You haven't been to the mainland."

"I have."

What? I try desperately to curb my anger and my disappointment, but it must show through my expression because Negunn's smile widens to consume the bottom half of his face. His brilliant teeth glow and his light purple tongue lasciviously licks his pink and gold bottom lip. It glistens like elstone in a way I wish mine would, but that's a stupid hope. I can't change my genetics any more than Negunn can change the fact that he's an asshole.

"Cera." I shake my head. "You don't even have a dulaha."

"I don't need one. The harvest has been big and they need any and all hands they can get." He nods. "I offered my assistance, showed them that I could make the First Leap and they brought me along. We've been harvesting reevi from the big island. A couple of the smaller ones too, but I went to the big island the last solar and, when I was there, I found something."

"What?"

"Wouldn't you like to know."

"Negunn..." I turn to face him, my shoulders tight and a sudden heat in between my shoulder blades flaring with rage. He doesn't reply. He doesn't even move. I take two steps forward and his gaze drops again to my chest, and then to my hips. This is dangerous, because if he looks at me like a creep for much longer, I might just believe him...

I stab my heel into the ground. "Negunn, those are our people. If we can help them, it's our obligation to."

"I'm a prince, Latanya. I have no obligations."

"You're a reevi harvester, Negunn. Your princely status means nothing here."

"You're wrong. What I have might just make me king."

"Negunn, we don't have kings. Not here and not on Quadrant One."

He shrugs, looking calm, not riled by my insults or statement of facts at all. "Prince or not, I still have something that you need and I don't believe in giving things away for free. That wouldn't be very…princely of me."

"I'm not raxing you in exchange for information…" I start to turn, rage rattling up my spine and into the base of my neck. It burns. I feel like crying. And I hate that above everything Negunn's successfully jammed a wedge between me and Grizz when we already have a wedge the size of the mainland shoved between us.

Why is Negunn able to explore the mainland? Cera — why *not* me? And is Negunn right? Maybe Grizz's odd and oddly sexual advances in the lunar aren't anything but a dulaha making clothes for his pupil. Maybe, in his gobbling dark green eyes, I really am a beast. You wouldn't get aroused if you accidentally touched a beast's genitals and so far, I've got no evidence that he has. I haven't seen his cock, let alone his erection. Not since that first time we were flying together.

"I don't need you to rax me, Latanya." He beams brilliantly, the rain doing nothing to dampen his glow. "Not yet."

Terrifying, that reply, but…he has all the tokens in this mok biz game that we're playing and he knows it. "What do you want?"

He doesn't answer. Not right away. Not until I turn to fully face him and, for the first time, he doesn't look down at my body. He stares directly at my face in a way that's even more unnerving than when he speaks to my breasts. "I want you to give me a kiss."

"Negunn…"

"Not on the mouth. Just on the cheek." He taps his perfectly round and flawlessly dimpled left cheek and I frown. This…doesn't seem right. But…it's much less than what I thought he'd ask for.

"I kiss you on the cheek and you tell me where to find the survivors?"

"You kiss me on the cheek and in three solars, when we take our next trip to the mainland to harvest another batch of reevi, I'll find them and tell you where they are. I don't want to get your hopes up until I'm sure."

A kindness. I don't trust it. And yet…even if I get nothing from it, a kiss is a small payment to waste. "You promise?"

"Shenti, Latanya. A little kiss on the cheek is all I want. Here, I'll even make it easy for you." He lowers to the ground and, in a surprising display of strength, maneuvers the stack of five or six reevi shoots to the ground beside him. Kneeling, he looks up at me like a male I don't recognize. One I might respect. It's an act, I know, but it's a clever one because when I feel like backing out, he looks up at me like this.

I take a tentative step towards him and the Thirst starts to let up. A good omen? Perhaps anywhere but on Revatu, where the Thirst itself is only seen as good. "Just the one kiss and just this one time," I confirm.

Negunn nods. "Shenti, Latanya." I don't know if he's baiting me by speaking in Revatu or not, but I also know that a kiss is a kiss. It doesn't have to mean anything and, with Negunn, it most definitely won't.

I breach the gap between us and quickly lean down and give him a swift peck on the cheek. I step back just as quickly and brace myself for the accusations I know are to come about how I've jipped him by giving him the handshake equivalent of a kiss. Instead, he gathers his reevi up onto his shoulder and tips his chin forward.

"See you in three solars, Latanya." And then he walks off, leaving me confused and wounded and a little... hopeful.

8

Grizz

Latanya is in a strange mood. She was angry with me earlier, but now she will barely look at me. I watch her swing from the platform's precarious edge off into the void where she dangles, suspended, before her hand snaps out and snags the next vine. She's getting better.

"She's getting better." Slascax stands beside me with her arms crossed over her bare chest. She wears full wraps on solars when she isn't hunting, and this solar, she isn't. I have a small team that will join me at the coming solarbreak as the Thirst prevents us from discerning much in its wake.

I nod.

"Have you decided whether she will join us on the coming hunt? She may be useful in the search for her people."

"Shenti."

"Shenti, she'll be joining us or shenti, you've decided?"

"The latter."

"And?"

"And she will not be joining us."

Slascax snorts. "You know they've taken N'gon across the divide already and he is barely as good a flyer as she is."

"Good. Better that he falls."

Slascax shakes her head, her loose hair slicking back away from her face and winding like a river over her shoulders, caught in the tempest of the Thirst and, in the mist it's left behind, drying slowly. My hair, half tied back from my face, undoubtedly looks much the same. Somehow, in the Thirst, Latanya's hair does not appear darker, but brighter. It makes my gut squeeze, seeing it — seeing her. She truly is a creature of Revatu. How she was ever lost from us, I'll never know, I just thank the stars she's been returned where she belongs.

Slascax is dogged as she says, "You know that doesn't matter. The cocorangee…"

"Shenti," I grunt, for the first time, reviling the accord we've set up with the cocorangee. Not that it matters. From what I've heard from the other harvesters, N'gon has not fallen yet. "He will meet his end when it is time."

Slascax nods and I don't like this at all. She should be rebuking me for such talk, and that she isn't can only mean she and I are in agreement where N'gon is concerned.

"Has he done something to you?" I can't help but ask, though I cringe to hear the answer.

"Cera."

"Has he said something? Have you heard something?"

"Cera. Only that he is well liked by the other harvesters, the females in particular."

A low, burning growl takes up residence deep in my chest, rather than my throat. Slascax's left brow — and the left side of her mouth — lift. She glances down at my neck and chest and I quickly try to cut the sound that it emits. Turns out, I cannot. Not when thoughts of Latanya are concerned.

"Have you told her yet that you think she might be the one to unleash your Hunger?"

I start, physically jolting at the accusation — and its accuracy. "How do you know this?"

"I didn't. Not until you just told me now."

I round on her, looking away from my deliha as she reaches the opposite platform and takes her rest. The distance is more than what she'd need to cross the divide and she has managed it for the second solar in a row, without falling. And with a surprising amount of speed for an amateur and an elegance even many seasoned flyers do not possess. She is a natural at this. *I should have let her accompany me solars ago.*

"Slascax, if you tell anyone, it would ruin everything."

She rolls her eyes and purses her lips around her tusks in a form of sneer that I hate and that she knows I hate. "I won't tell anyone, though you should tell *her*, at least."

"She wouldn't understand."

"Tell her about Mornar. Have him demonstrate for her."

I balk, and then laugh a booming, yet hollow laugh. "You think that showing her what I might become *for her* would convince her of my suitability as her mate?"

She gives me a peculiar look. "Why wouldn't it? One of only two males with a beast form certainly is recommendable to any female searching for a mate."

"She isn't searching for a mate. She searches for her kin — kin I have yet to find for her." And she seeks sex — something any male can provide, and I don't want to be any male to her, but the *only* male. "I've done nothing to prove myself."

Slascax nods, knowing I'm right. "You shouldn't have taken her for a deliha," she says after a lengthy pause. Together, we watch Orick on the far platform give Latanya additional tips to help her move laterally instead of forward, should a vine in front of her break.

"I couldn't let another male get that close."

She scoffs. "Males..." Before she has a chance to complete her insult, I hear a yelp.

Latanya falls in a blink, the vine she'd been clinging to slipping from the tree above and tumbling down. She attempts the maneuver Orick taught her a moment ago, but she isn't fast enough. She plummets towards the net and I quickly launch myself into the obstacle course and slide down the full length of the first vine I come to. I land on the thick netting just as Latanya finishes rolling to one side and starts to amble off of it.

I jump down after her, landing on the soil, which remains hard beneath the moss despite the Thirst that's drenched it. "Latanya, are you alright?"

"Shenti. Shenti," she repeats, nodding absently as she twists her arm from side to side. I move to cut her off and reach for her hand, which she promptly pulls away from me.

"There are bruises on you arm from the netting — you must have fallen on it wrong. I told you to land on your back..." I reach for her arm a second time and she swats my hand as hard as she can.

"Grizz. Stop it. It's not…from the net. It's from…" She pauses, something elusive shifting in her expression like a vine that I can't grab onto. "Earlier."

"With Privanka?" I clench. That doesn't make sense.

"Cera. Just…leave it alone. Leave *me* alone." Her lips flutter and she shakes her head, her stare never leaving the ground between our feet. There's nothing there, though, and she doesn't seem to be as concerned with the bruising on her arm as she should be. Against her dark skin, even darker streaks show.

Rejected. I've been rejected by my mate. I take an immediate and painful step forward while streaks of tension web across my chest. "Latanya, I…"

"Enough, Grizz." My throat dries as I watch the tips of her glowing white hair flutter in the next strong wind.

My throat dries and I'm overcome with an emotion too strong to keep in. I let it burst from my lips, "Latanya, I'll take you to the mainland. This coming solar, I'll take you."

What am I doing? Begging like a spoiled child for the smallest ounce of her approval? I just want to see the small smile in her expression return, or the way her eyes round and her eyelashes flutter as she absorbs my every instruction. I want to see the relaxing of her body in my presence and, more than all of this, I want to know that I haven't made that up. It is the ultimate reward, and one I'm not eager to spoil. But right now, my offer…it has the opposite effect.

She freezes. She doesn't meet my gaze, but turns her head to the side so that I can see her face in profile. "But…I fall…fell."

"Everyone falls. It's how you fall that matters and you fall with courage and grace."

She closes her eyes and her nostrils flare. She shakes her head. "You only…want me to come…because I'm mad at you…and you want me."

"Cera." The word punches out of me on a growl. I close the distance between us completely and dwarf her height, drowning her in my shadow. Her back tenses against my chest. She sucks in a short, tight breath and doesn't move. "I…" *I do want you.* "I am your dulaha and I don't want to see you hurt. This is why I haven't taken you to the mainland. But you earned the right to go. You can cross the divide. You took the First Leap solars ago. I should have taken you then."

"So…you don't want me?" The tenderness of her question is enough to raise my beast from its sleep.

"Latanya…" I growl violently enough to make her jump. She steps away from me, but I gently slide my hands around her hips and pull her closer. I'd like nothing more than to bend her over my knee and tan her lovely hide before rutting her into oblivion, but there is a void between us no vine is long enough to reach.

"I…I'm sorry. I should…should not have said…"

"Latanya. I'm not *allowed* to want you. I'm your dulaha. It is not my job to lust after you, but to serve you…"

"What if this is how I want you to serve me?"

Rackes. Rackes me to the center of the Mouth. Burn me alive for eternity. "In time, I can court you." Once I kneel to her, and she presents me with a token of her affection. An article of clothing, a tender touch, a hug, even a kiss. "Until then, this will have to be enough."

"Well, it isn't." Her small fists clench and she wrenches away from me and the Thirst just as suddenly decides to have its revenge and growls out a bellowing thunder. Wind whips through the treetops, carrying her sweet scent to me. She smells of salt, like the sea, and like the elgar flowers that grow from its essence, clinging to the vines that web across the sides of the cliff. She smells like she belongs to me.

"You say serve, so *serve*." Her gaze flashes down to her feet. "On your knees."

The challenge strips me bare and flays me alive. There is no possible way I cannot respond to it, not least of all because I see the glow of disappointment reflected to me in the white and brown of her eyes. What is this? Where did it come from? This vulnerability? This angst? This petulance? This...this desire for me and the affection I'm denying her.

I frown severely while her gaze flits between my eyes. Finding nothing of value there, clearly, she starts to turn, but I can't rackesing have that. I stoop towards the ground, press my shoulder into her stomach and lift her high onto my shoulder without ever breaking stride. She yelps, but I don't release her as I make my way through the Thirst and across the convening square where so many of my people watch me carry Latanya past.

"Grizz!" Nevo shouts, attempting to catch me. I raise a hand. I do not have time for her or whatever she has to say to me now.

My inner beast is raging, thirsting, needing, begging to be let free. If only I knew how to let it. I imagine it would not be so difficult if I merely undid the latch to my knowledge of what is right and wrong here on Revatu and did whatever I wanted. *Why can't I? She isn't even from here.*

I recoil from the thought, as tempting as it is, as I slip into the thickness of the trees, finally finding the one with the grooves notched out of the side in three parallel lines at hip level. The sign demarcating my home. Our home. *Her* home.

I yank on a vine overhead and a short ladder tumbles down. I climb without releasing Latanya until we're inside my home, the trap door shut and barred beneath us. In the center of my serving room, I set her down.

She's breathing hard, her fists are clenched and she's having trouble meeting my gaze as I slowly lower to the ground before her, taking to both knees. "I…shouldn't have said…what I said," she pieces together, using her translator to do most of it. And yet, she uses words that I have taught her, too. "You don't…have to do…"

I grab her behind the knees and wrench her forward, burying my nose in her covered crotch, where the scent of her is sweetest. She mewls loudly, the sound bare in its most primal form. My cock hardens instantly, or maybe it was already hard from before. From the moment she woke the lunar previous, pretending to sleep while I measured her form. Perhaps, from the moment I first laid eyes on her and gathered her into my arms.

My claws move up the outsides of her legs, which tremble in ways I find absolutely delightful. Her desire jacks up my breathing and my stomach and back muscles pull together, as if trying to contain something eager and lethal. I exhale onto her bare stomach as I cut through the laces along the front of her pants and drag them down in one motion.

My eyes widen as I take in the sight of her sex, the cords of my throat straining as I release a low rumble. I have seen her bare before but not like this. Never dripping… "You're hurting, my Latanya."

"Mhmm." She grabs onto my left shoulder and tries to squeeze her thighs together, blocking the sight of that slick-soaked cunt from my gaze. I slide my hands between her thighs, struggling to keep my claws in check, and pry her legs apart. "Auwh… Grizz…" She sounds afraid.

She should be afraid.

"I'm a terrible dulaha, aren't I, for letting you suffer like this?" I breathe hot air onto the patch of her black curls and her knees both simultaneously buckle. I catch her around the curve of her ass with both of my hands and pull her forward.

Her knees bump against my chest and I feel how they shake. I feel it in my heart and the rapid way it beats. I feel it in my chest, how it vibrates like the Thirst itself. Does she feel the way my beast purrs for her? She must. The whole rackesing house feels poised to shake apart around us.

I inhale deeply, her elgar flower scent. Her precious mound glistens with a Thirst of its own and, when I part her folds with my thumbs, she releases a garbled sound, her eyes roll back and her pretty cunt weeps.

I dive forward, pressing my tusks against her mound so that it puckers perfectly into my mouth, which I open wide enough to lavish all of her. I taste each of her folds, nibbling and licking her clean before moving on and spearing her with my tongue where she's hottest and where she needs me most.

"Grizz," she shrieks, grabbing a fistful of my hair in a way I'm not sure she's conscious of, but that I *love*. It feels like a claiming.

I purr louder for her, my beast satisfied with such a claim — as am I. I lick her harder to reward her, laving my tongue over her again and again, careful to catch her as she sways from side to side, torso arching in a backward bend. "Grizz, ohmystars," she breathes what sound like curses in her own tongue, "rax… ohcometsthisfeelssogood…"

Pleased by her adulation, I finally give her what she seeks. I lift my tongue just a little, lips moving carefully in coordination, and I suck her small, softest skin in between the hard fangs of my teeth. She screams and her muscles fail her. I catch her and carefully lower her to the wooden floor of my home without unlatching my mouth from around her dripping wetness. She's a river rushing wild, gushing down my throat. The taste of her is stunning and overwhelming and everything I ever hoped for.

She tries to close her legs around my face, but I spread her thighs open and continue to feast. She writhes. Her body makes wonderful, beautiful sounds and shapes. I reach up and tear my claws through the front of her shirt, ruining the bindings over her breasts as I free them to my gaze. I…didn't exactly mean to do that, but I'm not sure how it could be helped at this stage.

I grab onto her right breast and watch in fascination as the soft, soft, soft nipple there peaks. Females of my species have hard nipples. They're hard everywhere, ready to brave Revatu's Hunger and its beasts. But she's so soft. *Too soft.* She could be hurt so easily across the divide, on the mainland. I should keep her here…but the longer I do, the more she reviles me for it.

My frustration surges, but it's as if she can read my thoughts and seeks to scrape them clean. Her fingers reach for me, blunt claws scraping my scalp, and she breathes, "Grizz, *rax* me."

A roar tears out of my throat and I prowl up her body. "I cannot," I tell her as I scrape my tusks over her flesh, licking and tasting her everywhere that Revatu's Thirst ever went.

"But...I want..." she says in my tongue, fighting for concentration as she fights to keep her eyes open. Her lashes flutter and so does her mouth. She rubs the center of her chest roughly as I bracket her head between my arms and loom over her. "I feel...feel strange...it...hurts." She gestures towards her sex and inadvertently rubs her hand over the front of my hides.

I hiss, the pressure brutal, and shake my head, lifting a little further off of her. "I'm no better than N'gon if I don't honor you first."

"You are...different. When...you ask...I say...shenti." Her eyes fill with a shocking surge of tears as she stares up at me and I must react because she quickly covers her eyes with one hand. "But...you don't ask." She pushes on my shoulder and I immediately relent and watch her wriggle out from beneath me. But instead of moving away from me, the evil temptress turns onto her belly and lifts up onto her hands and knees, presenting her weeping cunt and perfectly puckered ass to me. A gift I haven't earned...but it tempts me so raxing greatly...

"Latanya, you may not feel this way," I start, voice nearly too thick to speak through, "and it may not dishonor you not to follow our traditions. But it dishonors *me*." And it frightens me. Because if I take her once, to her it may mean just that. But to me? To me it means eternity. I want to *mate* her, not only to mate with her. To tell her that now...I worry it will frighten her off.

She whimpers and pushes her ass towards me, her breasts swinging in a way that makes me eager to latch onto them. I find myself kneeling behind her before I realize I've moved, my covered hips pulsing shallowly against her bare ass, my mound straining at the ties of my hide.

"But I *need*. I feel…" She shakes her head and runs a hand back through her hair — a look of frustration if I've ever seen one. It hurts me, because I can feel her need… at least, in part. But I wonder if she doesn't somehow feel *more*. *Xiveri…* The thought hits me with unnerving force, less like a hope and more like a premonition.

On Revatu we have known of Xiveri for most of our remembered history. Geeri wasn't the first Voraxian to crash land here. Several came before her and, when they arrived, some felt a draw, intense as gravity, to members of our community — in one case, to each other. In Geeri's case, it didn't come upon her suddenly, but over time. But if my Latanya is perhaps of a shared species that feels Xiveri with crushing force, what if I am denying her *her* tradition for the sake of mine?

What if it hurts her?

"Grizz, *please. I…ache.*"

"Rax," I snarl, unsure in ways I'm usually not. *Frightened, too.* I don't want to do the wrong thing. But it seems as if every action I take or don't take is wrong for her. I palm her left cheek, kneading it firmly, and retract my claws. I lock in on a decision — a tentative middle ground — and then enter her throbbing core with my middle finger.

"Grizz…" She moans, thrusting back on my hand.

I withdraw my hand and slap her ass lightly, but enough to make her jolt. "You'll take what I give you." Because if she needs much more, I might fully unravel. "Isn't that right, Latanya?"

"Shenti," comes her whispery reply. She settles, but it's a farce. I can see the way her clawless hands clutch the red woven carpet. *Red. She looks raxing lovely in red.*

I thrust two fingers inside of her roughly and she responds with a moan that is pure satisfaction and makes my beast purr triple-time. I penetrate her again and again, sweat beading on my forehead as I fight against the most threadbare tether.

My other hand snakes around her body to find her small folds, the ones that hide the delicious center of her pleasure. She shocks me by combusting on the lightest touch. Her body slouches forward, but I know better than to believe she's finished. I pick her limp, shivering form from the floor and carry her to the bed where I relieve her of her ache again and and again and again.

9

Latanya

I wake in a daze, like I went out heavy drinking the lunar before. I'm not even sure it is lunar. Candles are lit all around the room. I can see Grizz in their soft glow.

He's lying on the bed beside me staring down at my naked body with a certain male satisfaction that makes me feel warm. Warm…and embarrassed. He's still got his pants on and there's no sign of an erection, if there ever was one.

I fight against the lethargy weighing me down and roll onto my side facing away from him. My arms shake as I push myself up into a seat and cover my breasts.

"Latanya, are you hungry? How do you feel? Can you walk to the relief room? I can carry you there…" His claws scrape my shoulder and I shiver, a little bit of my fever coming back. I grit my teeth and fight against it, snaking out from under his touch.

"I'm fine."

I awkwardly amble to the edge of my bed — *the* bed — and drop my feet over the side. My feet are all tingly. My bones are all tingly. They *hurt*. I don't feel right.

"Latanya, what's wrong?"

I shake my head, feeling near tears at the calm and control he's exhibiting right now. I feel so *lonely*, so needy, so desperate. I feel raxing pathetic. And yet, none of that matters. My heart is still pounding with the want I have for him and I want so raxing much. "Do you think…think I'm…like a beast?"

Dry warmth comes against my back, a contrast to the humidity against my front, where I feel damp and chilly and exposed. "Shenti. You're my little monster." His lips come down onto my shoulder and I nearly implode under the touch. I curl my shoulders tightly forward and I feel, rather than see, as he pulls back. "You don't like my attentions?"

"You think…I'm ugly."

"Sesiva'a?"

"You think I'm ugly…like a beast."

A growl rips out of his throat, so loud and hard it makes me jolt. His hand clamps onto my shoulder and this time, he doesn't let me go when I try to pull away from him. He yanks me onto my back. "Latanya, you think I find you ugly?"

Flat on my back on the bed, I push up onto my elbows and try to crawl backwards away from him. My head clunks against the headboard and I reach up to rub it. Distracted as I am, I don't react in time to avoid him grabbing onto my ankles…and spreading my legs around his knees as he continues to kneel before me and rake his gaze up and down my body. I shudder. So exposed. Grabbing a pillow and covering my front with it, I nod.

Grizz snarls, his tusks flashing in the flickering candlelights. "Does it look like I find you ugly?"

I'm not sure. I don't know what the glow in his eyes means, or the glow in the back of his throat. I shrug.

Grizz releases my left ankle and rips open the hide covering his crotch. He reaches down...down...and holy stars...I didn't notice the bulge before because I thought it would be pushing at the leather strips. Instead, he tucked it down his left leg and it takes quite a lot of maneuvering it for him to be able to free it.

My stars... His cock is huge — easily the biggest one I've ever seen. My mouth waters and a sharp, slicing pain cuts through my pelvic muscles. I try to slam my legs shut, but Grizz holds them open, slips his hands underneath my knees and yanks.

He shifts forward on his knees and covers my body with his. I gasp as his huge, veiny, *unusually*-shaped cock presses against my mons, and then flutters over my clit. He drags it down and the strange flaps? scales? something — I don't know what they are — scrape roughly over my sensitive flesh. He reaches down between us and everything in me clenches, wondering, fearing, anticipating the moment that he finally pushes inside...

But he doesn't.

He reaches between us and uses his thick thumb and pointer finger to spread my lips apart, then he rubs the rounded head of his cock through my folds. His face is a mask of concentration, but he never breaks, except maybe in the flaring of his nostrils. He's perfectly in control.

"Does it feel like I find you ugly?"

"But you don't...come in." I sniffle.

He freezes. He yanks me down the bed further and climbs on top of me, resettling himself so that his cock is pressed against my bare stomach. His hands cradle my face, his eyebrows drawn furiously over his nose. "Latanya, I want you *desperately*." His voice cracks and it's in that crack that I find what I've been searching for this entire time.

Hope.

"But you…I look…" It takes so long for me to find the words, I push against his shoulders and release a short hiss of frustration.

"Cera. You cannot run from this." He grabs my wrists and slams them down on the bed. "Now, tell me in your words. I don't care how long it takes. Why do you think I don't want you?"

"Because you don't enter!"

"Latanya!" His voice is a contained shout that slaps me silent. "I don't enter because I don't want you *once*. I want you *forever*. And I can't take you because I haven't complied with the mating rituals of Revatu."

"I…but…but…but I look…"

His gaze is hooked on my mouth and, before I can finish speaking, he presses his lips to mine in a kiss that can only be described as bruising. His tusks crush my mouth and chin but when he parts his lips, he uses his much softer tongue to caress my bottom lip gently. Oh so gently. My back arches up and my breasts find his bare chest. *Rax, it feels so good…*

"Grizz," I moan, my nipples scraping his rough chest, my arms straining against the hold he has on them. He's so much stronger than I am. So much more powerful. I love that difference, but I also love knowing that, at any point, this is a position I could get out of. That he would let me out of.

I don't feel that way with Negunn.

My face heats in a sudden sensation, like I've left the gas on too long before the igniter catches and my whole body is engulfed in a poof of flame. Sweat ripples down my spine and I fight against it — whatever this is — at the sound of Grizz softly saying my name.

I open my eyes and see that he's on his side. I'm on mine. We're facing each other and he has his arms wrapped around me. Pillows are stacked under us, but my head still rests on his folded elbow. His face is a mask of concern, hard cheeks stone bricks, wells of his eyes deep enough to cast shadows, ruthless gaze glittering with suspicion.

"I may have made my interest unclear, and for this I'm sorry." His hand strokes down my cheek to my shoulder. He pulls the blanket up from my waist to further cover me. "Here, on Revatu, permission must be requested before the tribe for a male or female to court another. Once permission on part of the intended mate is given, the courting process begins and, eventually, if satisfied, the mate asks for a tre'or'oro, a final gift or demonstration of affection. Once the tre'or'oro is procured and accepted, the mated pair celebrates their union before the tribe, with the tribe.

"I...circumvented the process. I...made a mistake. From the first moment I saw you, I felt a connection to you that I could not deny. I believe you may be linked to me, capable of transforming me into...a great warrior." He seems to struggle with his own vocabulary, which doesn't make sense. He knows I can understand.

But I don't understand and shake my head. "What do...what great warrior?"

"Mornar is one such...warrior. He can...transform. His ability only began when Geeri arrived, crashed onto

Revatu much in the same way you did. She was a Voraxian spice trader and was traveling alone when she crashed. She accepted a dulaha — one that wasn't Mornar — while Mornar engaged her in courtship. Eventually, she accepted Mornar for a mate. He courted her the *proper* way, but I didn't. I couldn't…let another male be your dulaha. I couldn't let you go to a home that wasn't mine. I'm not a good male, but a possessive and jealous one when it comes to you…"

I smile, albeit feebly as this information crashes down onto me like a storm. "I think…you are…a good male. And I feel this…connection to you, too."

A rumble picks up in Grizz's chest. He looks down at my own chest and strokes a claw between my breasts. It sends my heart into a frenzy and my lust into overdrive. I whimper out a moan and Grizz pulls his hand away. Ugh. So raxing frustrating… "Maybe. Or maybe, you only find me beastly enough to rut once."

"That's not true!" I practically shout the words. His eyes flare. Heat fans the flames of my desire, transforming it into another disappointed rage. "You are not ugly…"

"Cera. I'm not. But neither are you. Who made you believe you are?"

My throat clamps. I don't like the direction this conversation has taken and I immediately attempt to retreat from it. "You are not ugly…"

"Latanya, you are as lovely as a fallen star. Why do you view yourself any differently?"

I exhale shakily, my chest still tight, even as the admission rolls off of my tongue awkwardly in patched together words and phrases. "I am…not like the others… of Quadrant One. My parents…adopted me?" I try, he nods, seeming to understand what I mean. "My mom is of Lemora…tall. She has horns. They became…white when she loved my dad."

"And he *is* of Quadrant One?"

I nod.

"Like N'gon?"

I nod again, lips twitching at his pronunciation of Negunn's name. But I don't correct him. Rax whatever the Revatu want to call him.

"Shenti…but not like Negunn. Negunn is…wretched. My father is kind. My mom…she knew instantly. My dad did not. He still…courted her? He let her love him. He…fell in love, too. Like Xiveri…but it took…time. And when they mated, he lost…lost his position for it. They don't like…others on Quadrant One."

"And you? Did they like you, Latanya?"

I shrug, though the answer is decidedly *cera*. "They were…kind enough. I thought males thought…I thought males liked me. But they just want…wanted to try…" I gesture at my body and a rough, brutish, *animalistic* sound huffs from between Grizz's tusks. It tastes like smoke, a recently stoked fire.

He slides one hand around the back of my neck and yanks me close. I think he's about to kiss me but with a breath separating us and a breath alone, he says, "I do not want a sample, Latanya, I want to mate you for *life*."

I suck in a breath, which he chases, kissing me hard and passionately enough for my toes to curl and my fists to clench. He doesn't give me more than that, though. Like waters on the shore, ebbing and retreating and ebbing again and again.

"Thank you for sharing this with me," he says. "I understand even better now why you worry for your kin. They showed you acceptance, didn't they?"

I nod, eyes watering as my mind flicks to them, and as I absorb the fact that he's understood something so *personal* about me in my short, stunted speech. "Shenti. They love me...unconditionally. They...make me feel... not so alone."

Grizz's anger doesn't die. In fact, his muscles tense. "You are not alone, Latanya. I feel it in my blood, in my bones, you belong here." He grabs my hand and places it on his chest.

My skin prickles all over, along every exposed stretch of my skin, and beneath that same sensation it travels along every nerve ending. I feel something moving beneath my breast and behind my eyes and Grizz gives me a curious look when I next blink. But, before he can say anything else and rip me open completely, I blurt, "What do you mean? Here...on Revatu? In your bed? Or..." I'm too embarrassed to say it, but I can see the expectancy in his gaze. He *wants* me to acknowledge this — whatever *this* is between us. "Or with you?"

"All of it, Latanya. All of it."

I bite my bottom lip while some beautiful, rich substance in my stomach surges up into my chest, like a fist made out of liquid gold. I open my mouth, certain I'll exhale smoke just like Grizz sometimes does. But... "But...how can you know...for sure?"

His palm crushes mine against his heartbeat even more fiercely, to the point that it almost hurts. "Because I feel for you, Latanya. I cannot yet define it, but I know that it is ancient and dangerous and that it has me, and will not let me go."

10

Grizz

I was feeling an enormous relief, like the cool balm of the Thirst after an explosive Hunger, as I watched Latanya finally drift to sleep the lunar before. We'd spoken deep into the lunar, sharing vulnerabilities that left me certain that Latanya would *likely* choose me for a mate if given the opportunity, but that that choice won't be possible until she feels safe, and she will never feel safe until she is certain of what happened to her kinfolk.

I sleep not nearly as long as I'd like after the lunar I had dreaming — cera, *replaying* — the tang of Latanya's sweet cunt dripping down my throat as she released orgasm after orgasm, a Thirst all her own. I wake with a throbbing erection and quickly slip out of bed and into the relief room, a moniker which takes on entirely new meaning as I stroke my cock to the memories of the lunar before.

I release beneath the stream of water that pours through the fountain overhead, splattering pale green across the wall. What's strange is that the mating barbs lining the shaft of my cock from below the head all the way down to my balls inflate immediately afterward. It's *painful* and a little disarming. They've never done that before, *ever*, not even after a good rut and here I am not even inside a female.

I stroke them down, releasing once more under the pressure of my hand and, after cleaning up the mess I've made across the reevi-shoot walls, I return to the bedroom to see Latanya sitting up, facing me.

I swallow hard, a little embarrassed that she may have heard me. I wasn't exactly subtle. "Do you need to bathe? There's still plenty of warm water."

"Cera."

I notice that she's rocking subtly back and forth and I frown. "Are you alright?"

"What's on the…what we do this solar? Mainland?"

Her words come out more stilted than they had the lunar before, like she's too distracted to properly translate the words coming through her translator and can't remember any of the words she knows. "Shenti. I need to show you something early this solar. Then after second meal, we will gather the hunters and go to the mainland and find your kin."

She nods and stands, turning quickly to face the baskets containing her clothes and mine. I have many more than she does, but that will change in no time. "Let go."

"Let go?" I smirk, prowling up behind her. "That is the number one thing *not* to do here on Revatu. You must always hold fast." I touch her shoulder, stroking a single claw over the knobs of her spine until they disappear beneath the blanket she's gathered around her.

"Don't!" She shrieks, staggering away from me. "Don't touch me."

"Sesiva'a?"

"I just…it…pain." She shakes her head, white strands falling like curtains on either side of her face. She doesn't look at me and she doesn't speak to me again as she quickly dresses and swallows down half the amount of food she needs and twice the amount of water and I'm left stunned, confused, and raxing *angry* as I descend the rope ladder after her.

"Are you sure you're capable of this?" I ask her as we step up to the edge of the divide and take hold of parallel vines. She looks woozy, feverish, dazed… "Latanya, you look unwell. Is it the food? Did you eat something?"

"Cera. Cera, it's not the food." She shakes her head and squeezes her eyes shut tight. She opens them and stares fixedly on the vine trapped between her dark brown hands. Beautiful hands that flex gorgeously in the solar's bright yellow light. "Not the food," she whispers again.

Her gaze flashes to me for the first time this solar and I see in her eyes the same thing I saw in them the lunar before. A brightness that I hadn't noticed before. I frown. "You have a fever. Your eyes are glassy. You should go home and rest. I will gather the hunters and head to the mainland now."

"Cera! You…you say…you *promised*." She closes her eyes and refocuses on the vine. My resolve is firming — she isn't ready this solar — until she says, "*Please,* Grizz."

"Augh," I growl, gripping the vine in one hand and turning to face the divide. A breeze ripples through my hair. It's unbound this solar as I forgot to tie it. I had… other things on the mind. "Follow me, but be prepared to stop halfway across."

She nods and, as the wind whips salty water up from the frothing ocean tide below, I leap. Sailing through the air, I can hear Latanya's small oomphs of exertion as she attempts to keep up. She is moving quickly this solar, but not as quickly as she usually does.

Worry kicks my sternum as I come to a stop halfway across the divide and wait for her to stop near me. Though she does, I notice that as we swing she chooses vines that take her further away from me. We should have been swinging side by side, as I always imagined swinging through the air with my future mate, but instead we're separated by enough vines to partially block sight of her face.

Frowning, I open my mouth, but she speaks first, keeping her eyes trained somewhere just shy of mine. Like she's staring at my throat. I watch hers contract, bobbing in a way my cock likes very much. "What now?"

"Let go."

"Sesiva'a?" She shouts over the sound of a particularly strong wind. Her vine swings, but she clings to it deftly, some of the fever seeming to clear from her gaze as she finally meets my eyeline, her gaze now filled with panic.

I grin. "Remember that rule about not letting go? This is the one time you'll need to ignore it."

"Cera! No way!"

"Just this once, Latanya. Let go."

"I'll die!"

I laugh. "I know you heard me this morning in the relief room. Do you really think I'd send a female that makes me ache like I've never ached before to her doom? Without even rutting her first?" I shake my head. "Trust that no male would. Or better yet, simply trust *me*." I meet her gaze and hold it and I wonder at the brighter brightness I'm seeing, almost like the whites of her eyes are expelling light onto her cheeks.

"Do you trust me, Latanya?"

She's nodding before she seems to have registered the question. Her expression has gone suddenly dazed. "Shenti," she whispers.

My heart squeezes like a fist in my chest and, when I speak, I exhale more than smoke this time. I taste *flame*. It licks at the back of my tongue, cool yet bright, like Latanya's eyes illuminating her face, but illuminating mine in a wholly different light.

"Then trust me, Latanya, and obey." When I speak, the words come out and don't resemble my voice in the slightest. They are too deep to belong to me — or anyone of Revatu — and so rumbly and rough as to be near unintelligible, but it doesn't seem to matter.

Latanya's eyes roll back into her skull, she closes them, she nods, and then she lets go of the vine with hands and feet and slips away.

I do not hesitate to follow.

We fall for long moments, long enough for me to open my eyes and see the frothing ocean waters reaching up, seeking to claim us. The web is clear, its lattice virtually invisible from up on the mainland, but as we descend closer and closer, I begin to make out the telltale pattern of its glistening shape. It turns the water a duller pink than it is in truth, but no foreigner would know this. And bringing Latanya here now is her final induction into our tribe. The secret only we Revatu know, a truce that must be brokered on behalf of the deliha by his or her dulaha. As I do for Latanya now.

It fills me with such pride, to be the one to show her our secrets. I want to know all of hers. I want her to know all of mine. *This is her home.*

Latanya hits the silk web instants before I do, her body bouncing wildly as I hit the lacy cocorangee silk a short stretch away from her. "Are you surprised?" I say, trying to clear my throat, but finding I can't. I roll to my knees and then to my feet. I'm well practiced at walking the silk, but it's still much more difficult than walking on firm land. I wonder if that's why Latanya hasn't yet moved…

"Latanya? Latanya!" Her eyes are closed and her back is arched. Her face is contorted in agony and her heels dig into the web like she's fighting an invisible, unknown adversary. In a single leap, I arrive at her side and drop down onto my knees. I slide my hand beneath her hair and cup the back of her head. Did she land wrong? Where is she injured? "Latanya, speak to me…"

The scent suckerpunches me, hitting me low in the gut and wrenching a bellow from deep within. The sound echoes through the canyon, accented by the sound of the waves crashing so close to us now. Latanya's eyes fly open and I jerk, my stomach pitching up into my chest, my heart leaping through the top of my skull. My lust hardening my thighs and spearing through the soles of my feet.

A grin spreads to consume my entire face, my entire raxing *being*. My body feels light as a feather, all but my balls, which feel like weighty stones. "Latanya," I sigh, watching her lips work to form words that don't come. There are no words. She has no need of them. "Latanya, you are *Voraxian*. You are my mate, but I am your Xiveri." Colors, a litany of them, pour from her eyes, filling every corner. The black pupil is gone. The brown is visible, but barely. And any uncertainty I had about her feelings towards me are erased.

"I…" Tears snake from her eyes, two of them falling in mirrored rivers.

I hiss, tongue clicking against the backs of my tusks as the deepest shame pulls at my male pride, unraveling it. "You are in the midst of the Xanaxana, the first mating. I've heard it feels different for everyone, some experiencing it slowly over time, others experiencing it in violence."

She tries to pull her legs together, squeezing them tight as if she has to pee so badly she'll explode. I know that isn't it, though, and reach between her legs, shoving her hands away from her crotch and cupping her core. She's damp, even through *hide*. I hiss. "And you are experiencing its fullest violence."

I quickly unlace my own hides, not caring where we are or who may be watching. I unlace the bindings over her breasts and spread her coverings, watch her breasts spring free, nearly black nipples forming hard peaks that beg to be sucked. I yank her trousers off.

I align my erection with her core, noting that the barbs along my cock are already inflating and deflating in small pulses, wanting to latch onto her, wanting to never let her go.

"Latanya, look at me." I attempt to command her attention, watch her lips work, watch her stare dart between my eyes, her breath coming harder and faster into her lungs. She's tearing apart. She's tearing *me* apart.

I feel a pang in my chest that pulses like a second heart and I nudge my cock forward, driving into a wet,

wet heat. "You are my mate, and I will not let you suffer through the Xanaxana alone. Are you ready?"

She mutters whispered gasps that don't quite manage to form words, but I take the way her nails claw the back of my shoulders and neck, pulling me down to her, as *shenti* nonetheless. I grin brutally, though I'm sure it looks more barbaric than reassuring. I'm about to unsnap and unleash havoc all over the place. *Or unleash more.*

"Then brace yourself, my little monster. I can't promise I won't be rough this very first time." I slam forward and she screams my name to the skies above.

//

Latanya

Grizz wasn't kidding — about any of it. He's rough. He's *everything*. He's my everything. My heart is beating so fast, I can't think, I can't see, I can't breathe. And he's rutting me so brutally, all I can do is lock my ankles at his lower back and hang on. He is wrong about one thing, though, I'm not Voraxian. I can't be. No Voraxian has ever looked like I do and I feel so manic I can't imagine any being in the known Quadrants has ever felt like this before.

But what about the colors? The sensation? Xiveri? The Xanaxana? The feeling that I'm linked to him irrevocably? The vision of him through the emotions blazing from my eyes?

Whatever I am, whatever this is, doesn't matter. All I know is the *rightness* I feel as he plunges his thick cock in and out of my body, the wet sound of our bodies slapping together making me leak even more wetness. His shaft is so rough as it enters and exits my heat again and again. His cock, from what I saw of it the lunar before, is lined in these V-shaped flaps — at least five around in at least as many rows — and occasionally it feels like they're *moving* inside of me. I don't understand…not until the first orgasm comes for me and

Grizz's face twists up in a mask of concentration as he soon follows.

He grabs the back of my neck and fists my hair with his other hand. His arms are fully cocooned around me and his legs are spread so wide that my legs can't spread any further. They burn at the hip flexors, but every time I try to resist, he spreads me open wider.

"Mine," he snarls against my mouth, his own mouth leaking smoke and — and is that fire? "Latanya *mine*."

My pussy walls clench at the word, as if summoned by a command my body knows already to respond to. "Grizz *mine*," I reply.

His cock seems to understand the mirrored command, too, because I feel it kick inside of me and then begin to move…something…*something* is happening. I try to look down, but Grizz's hold on my hair is completely immobilizing. My chin is tipped up so that I can't look anywhere but at his face, into his eyes.

"What…" I start to say in a whispered panic as the embers I've seen glowing in his gaze shine just a hair brighter.

"Don't move…barbs latching," he grunts, thrusting much more shallowly now.

Something *wonderful* and slightly *painful* fills my pussy when Grizz stops moving entirely. His head kicks back and his tusks jut out as he releases a roar that echoes back to me and causes my thighs to quiver and my pussy to convulse even harder. I scream as an unexpected orgasm rolls through me, my pussy squeezing as I feel him empty inside of me. Thoughts and consequences are irrelevant at this point. I just want *more*.

"More," I moan, freeing one of my hands from between our bodies and reaching up to grab his neck. My fingers don't coil all the way around, but I still squeeze hard enough to get his attention.

He looks down at me and the dark green of his gaze is another color entirely — red, to match the color of his claws. Fire flames out of his mouth, but it's cool against my cheeks as he speaks. "Can't let you go..." His arm squeezes me tighter.

Tears swim to my eyes as I feel a sudden rush of safety swamp me. "Don't."

"Can't stop..."

"Don't."

"Must," he chokes and, when he blinks, his eyes do something strange — even stranger. They become larger and more diamond-shaped and his pupils, they slit.

"Why?" I moan.

"I've...had...my...turn..." He looks down between our bodies, raising himself up just enough that I can see something alarming enough to cut a peep hole through the haze of my need, my desire and my acceptance. My belly appears swollen slightly around the outline of his cock, like my organs have been rearrange to accommodate him. And he looks bigger than I remember. Much, much bigger. In a momentary panic, I jerk up, but pain pinches my lower half and rattles through my pelvis.

"Grizz!"

Grizz releases my head and hair and grabs my hips so quickly his hands move in a blur. He holds me still. "Can't...release...barbs are inflated. I'm latched...and now he...wants...his...turn..."

"Wh...Sesiva...a..."

Grizz starts to *change*. His body lifts off of me and suddenly his stomach inflates, rounding smoothly in a way that freaks the stars out of me. "Grizz!"

"Don't…be…af…afraid…" His head — his *skull* — breaks apart and reshapes itself, forming a huge snout the size of my whole body. I gasp when I should have probably screamed, but Grizz looks down at me and blinks. "Trust…me… Warrior is…coming…"

My pussy squeezes. His eyes squeeze shut. And then he shoots up five bodies' lengths.

Grizz *transforms*, shifting into a beast. Is…is *this* the warrior he spoke of? The one only Mornar — and now Grizz — can transform into? As inconceivable as it seems, I know in my bones that it is. And I feel…as I watch him break apart, unmaking and making himself anew in this new *beastly* form, that this is a beast that I've met before…

Maybe in some previous lifetime.

Or more than one.

And I've loved him desperately in all of them.

His legs and arms shift, extending and forming massive, torso-sized hands and feet. His red claws remain, though now they're the length of a femur, each. His belly smooths and rounds and scales flake over his skin, all of them rough and glittery and green. I'm so overwhelmed, I can't decide what it is I'm seeing…And then I see *wings*.

Green wings unfurl from a spine that exists somewhere high above me. I can't see around his belly, trapped as I am beneath it, bracketed by weighty arms and unusually bent legs, pinned by the cock still inside of me. It hasn't grown more than it already did and for that I'm plenty grateful.

I'm breathing hard as I stare up and watch the long neck elongate even further, head twisting towards the sun while the net beneath us dips. "Grizz!" I squeak as I start to slip. I try to hold onto the net underneath me, but when I do, it pulls on his cock inside of me and pain flares hot and deep.

His tusks are the only recognizable thing about him, though now they fit neatly in his mouth as if they were always meant to belong in this face and it's his *other* face that's the transformation. *Nice to see you again,* I can't help but think as he twists his long, serpentine neck to look down at me. His translucent wings blot out most of the sun, tinging everything beneath them green as they beat.

Wind melts over me gently, while it thrashes the net brutally. His claws dig into it and I feel and hear as several *important* strands tear. "Grizz!" I scream for the hundredth time in as many heartbeats.

One massive clawed hand slips between me and the netting and lifts. Everything lifts. Everything but the net beneath me. I'm suddenly floating, impaled on a monster cock, while the wings above the beast lazily beat. He must have a wingspan that's half the length of the divide. We rise and I yelp and the claws tighten around me.

I grab onto him, but both of my arms wrap only around one finger. My full hand clutches one edge of one claw. I'm fully reclined on his palm, its length so long I can rest my head and my hips on it. Only my shins dangle in the air as we rise up higher…and higher… skirting out from beneath the hanging course of vines overhead and then moving above them, towards the clouds, towards the sun.

He raxes me in the sky.

I moan as the beast roars out a breath of vibrant red flame and, at the should-be-alarming sight, I feel my hammering heartbeat start to slow into something less frenetic and more lustful. Want that I'm powerless against returns to me as his cock deflates enough for it to be able to slide into and out of my body. It feels… incredible, except that I don't like the angle. I can't move. Grizz can only use me like a toy, impaling himself inside of me while I lay motionless. I whimper and the slight sound causes the winged beast's ear flaps to perk.

He stops rutting me and we fly, moving away from the curtain of vines, away from Revatu and towards the mainland. We don't fly long, but land in some kind of clearing. I can't see anything but his great underbelly. That is, until he turns me around. He drops me and I land on all fours, his slick cock slipping out of me easily, though it doesn't last long.

I've barely gotten myself upright on the soft, thick moss when I feel the beast's smooth underside graze my ass and lower back. I look up and see red claws spear the earth, fists ripping out shrubs by the root. I look back and see his feet disappear into thick foliage. I feel a nudge against my ass — a cock, hard all over again, seeking entry.

I reach beneath my body, finding the familiar cock bobbing between my legs. Familiarity soothes me and makes the haze return. I'm whimpering and needy as a spike of pain returns to my chest and, when I look down, I can see multicolored lights shining against my hands and arms. Is this what Grizz meant? Because it looks as if the light could only be coming from *me*.

I've only just gotten the head of Grizz's cock centered to my pulsing, painful pussy when he presses forward. He reenters me and a rattling shakes my entire body. I hallucinate that it's him for a moment, until I realize that it's me. I throw my head back and scream.

"Grizz…"

A growl fills my ears and is all I can hear. There is no more ocean. There are no more birds, insects, or predators. There is only this. Him and his beast and this magic coursing between us. And to think I ever thought myself beastly. Or that beastly could be bad.

I smile as my orgasm recedes enough for me to be able to feel him latching inside of me again. I drop onto my forearms, struggling to keep myself upright when one of his huge forward arms — legs? — lifts from the soil and slides underneath my body. His finger feels like the skin of a snake covered in fine grains of sand as it rubs over my breasts and then trails down to my stomach. I look down in alarm as I see my belly swollen in ways that don't look natural. I jolt forward, but he holds me in place with a growl that sounds so very, very like Grizz.

Holding me in a strangely gentle grip, he keeps me in place for what feels like forever. Long enough for some of my clarity to return and for another orgasm to wriggle out of me slowly, sweetly almost. I press my forehead to the moss, its coolness a blessing as I wait for my dragon mate to finish coming.

Moments pass, so many of them, long enough for me to find this situation both hilarious and heart-warming, before the dragon releases a final burst of fire to the skies and slips his now slightly less swollen erection free of my heat. I collapse forward onto his hand and he pulls me up with him as he takes to the skies again.

Dipping below the vine-laced curtain, we return to the net strung across the divide where he drops me beside my clothing. I'm not really sure what I'm expected to do with them given that there's light green semen covering the insides of both of my legs from hip to heel — that, and the fact that I've lost use of both of my arms. So, I just lie there staring up at the dragon beast as it writhes in the air, looking down at me momentarily before it seems to come to some sort of decision. The arms and legs shrink first, and then the head. The belly goes next and then the wings collapse back against the spine and it plummets to the net beside me.

I shriek as I vault up into the air, arms and legs windmilling before I drop back down with one bounce, but not two. On the second bounce, hands snatch me from the air and pin me to the warbling net. One hand fits itself to my left breast while the other grabs me by the back of the neck.

"Latanya." He kisses me, tongue invading my mouth as I gasp. "Thank you," he moans, "for accepting me…in all my forms."

I grab the tips of his hair and yank hard, kissing him back just as ferociously. I lick a line up his lower tusk and break the battle of our lips and tongues just long enough to breathe, "Thank you for…accepting me…in mine."

Grizz's eyes are bright, the green swirling with orange now like molten lava, orange but not black like their Hunger. His mouth opens as he pulls back and he shakes his head, like he's at a loss for words. "I did not quite expect that's how my first transformation would go."

I burst out laughing, unable to help myself. The sound is so…alien to me now, after so many solars spent worrying. I know I'll go back to that soon, but for now it feels so good. Like the purest relief. I don't feel so alone. And I don't feel alone at all when he starts to laugh with me.

We laugh together for so long a burst of crashing waves speckles my spine, making me jolt. I laugh harder at that, and Grizz rolls us over, so that he's on the bottom and I'm on the top. He kisses me again for many, many moments, until he's the one to pull back. "You know, I actually had a reason to bring you here…"

"Shenti? What is it?"

"There are some beings I would like you to meet."

A sound — much louder than even the waves — causes me to lift my head. My jaw drops as a creature clicks its way towards us. Grizz stands, fully nude, and pulls me with him even though I can't really walk on the net and I have no desire at all to walk towards this creature.

Ten times more terrifying than the dragon I just rutted, it's *huge* and a very, very unfortunate translucent white, which makes it look like a walking cloud — a look that is in strong contrast to the rather lethal way it comports itself, what with its snapping claws and hundreds of legs. No. Nuh uh. I am *not* about any of this.

"Grizz," I squeal, legs wobbly for more reasons than one.

He scoops me up off of the net and takes a few more steps forward, clicking *back* at the creature as it comes towards us, all of its thousands of spindly legs working out of time with one another. I glance behind it and realize it's not alone. They aren't alone — this creature is *clearly* sentient — as dozens or maybe hundreds of its friends appear in holes in the cliff face I hadn't noticed before. It's hard to tell exactly how many of them there are with how amorphous their shapes are and with their homogenous coloring.

I can almost feel their awareness touch me even though they have no discernible eyes or nose or mouth as Grizz clicks at the creature and then gives me a slight bounce in his grip. He says my name, followed by, "And Latanya, these are the cocorangee. They are led by Romangrinth."

"Uhm…hi?" I offer lamely.

Grizz makes a clicking sound that I struggle to repeat. It's clear that my translator does not recognize this language. It makes me think momentarily of Negunn and how out of his depth he'd be down here with these creatures.

I reply with a smile. When I get it mostly right, Romangrinth replies with the same series of clicks. I nod shakily at the creature. Grizz nods and continues to speak until eventually, Grizz laughs and Romangrinth and his…tribe return to the mountain and Grizz carries me away from the inhospitable mainland towards the safety of our island, Revatu, where a single vine extended down waits.

"We have a deal with the cocorangee. They give us free use of their web in exchange for periodic sacrifices."

"Web?" I squeak, suddenly very, very disturbed by the sight of a white ball eerily my size near the edge of the net as we approach the vine.

"Shenti."

"We…just have sex…had sex on their web?"

"Shenti." Grizz grins and rumbles a sound of pure satisfaction. He meets my gaze and I cannot help but feel victorious. "Romangrinth told me that, when you first fell, he wondered if you were a sacrifice. He said it became clear very quickly that you were not. He offered his congratulations on our mating, instead, but apparently we owe him an extra sacrifice or two for the damage we did to his web."

"We? *You!* Your…giant beast!"

"You liked my giant beast," he says, raising a brow as if in challenge.

I feel my face heat. "Shenti."

He growls as he takes the vine in one hand and tosses me over his shoulder. I squeal as he begins to climb up while carrying me. "Good. Because I plan to have you again. And so does he."

He swats my ass and I jolt on a squeal, my chest feeling light, even as all the blood rushes to my face. I'm not worried though, as I watch the web move further and further away until I can no longer discern it at all. All I can see is a periodic sheen when the light hits it just right, and all I can feel in my chest as my torso swings like a pendulum is that I trust him. The dragon orc.

The beast.

"What was that for?"

"For fun." He turns his head and bites my ass cheek and I squeal again, kicking my feet. He pauses in his ascent and firms my legs to his chest with one hand. "Careful, or I will have to punish you when we return from the mainland."

"You…made that…promise before."

"And I plan to keep it. But first, we'll find your kin and procure our sacrifice to the cocorangee."

"Has Negunn met…cocorangee?"

"Cera. He has not yet become one with the tribe. He has no dulaha. He has yet to prove himself trustworthy." That fills me with absolute glee and I smile as I pinch Grizz's backside. He swats my ass in return and says, "Why do you think of him now?"

"I don't think his…translator will work…with them."

"Probably not. They don't speak in words but in suggested feelings. It takes a long time for us on Revatu to learn their tongue. We learn it as kits. You likely won't ever master it. But you still haven't answered my question. I don't like that you're thinking of Negunn while you're covered in my cum."

I grin. "You should…I think Negunn could be… sacrifice."

Grizz laughs. "But I thought I was meant to disembowel him?"

"Hm," I consider in all seriousness. "Maybe both?"

"Both it is, my little monster."

12

Grizz

I exist in a euphoric state of complete and utter disbelief as I make my way back up to Revatu with Latanya, my mate, firmly in my grip. Cera, not just my mate, but my Xiveri mate, my one true mate, just as I am hers.

Her colors glowed for me and I am certain, judging by the surprise in her eyes, that she has never emoted like this before. Just as I have never before transformed, I did so for her and she did so for me. And the way she took me, *raxxxxx...* She dropped to all fours and presented for a monster a hundred times her size and she let him rut her just as he wanted — as I wanted — as I felt everything through his skin and saw everything through his eyes.

Rax.

She is perfect. And perfect for me.

There is no more doubt in my mind.

"Come, let us announce our mating to the tribe." I hold out my hand as we descend from our home, clean in a way that I loathe. I'd have much rather paraded her cum-encrusted body before the tribe just so they know how thoroughly my beast and I marked her and, through the scent of her sweetness all over my cock and face, how thoroughly she has marked me.

Latanya wasn't such a fan of that idea. Much to my chagrin.

"They won't be…mad anymore that we didn't do things…correctly?"

"Xiveri supersedes all."

Her eyes glitter as she looks up at me and takes my palm in hers. She lifts it to her lips and kisses the back of my green hand. The contrast against her own coloring makes my mind spin with thoughts of what could be — what *will* be — when we produce kits of our own. Though, it is early for this. I will need to speak with her about her plans and our plans and what we plan for our future. I will also need to tell her about the off-worlders…

"Grizz!" Slascax's voice precedes the sound of her crashing through the woods.

"Is that Sla?"

I smirk, enjoying the name she's chosen for *Sla*, just as I enjoy her calling me Grizz. "Shenti." I pitch my voice louder. "Slascax, we are here."

Slascax bursts through the foliage before us and, on her next inhale, her eyes widen. This pleases me greatly. "It looks like we didn't do a thorough enough job of cleaning ourselves off," I smirk.

Latanya slaps my stomach with the back of her hand. "Sla, are you okay?"

"Me? I'm okay, but you… oh cera…" She shakes her head and approaches with a peculiar expression.

I hold up my free hand, the other gripping Latanya's as we make our way forward, hoping to soothe her. There will be consequences to this, but I want her to be assured that nothing will happen to her. Xiveri cannot be contained or controlled.

"Slascax, calm yourself. Latanya has done nothing wrong and any blame there is to be had is mine and mine alone."

"Blame?" Latanya pipes up. "Cera blame!"

I smirk, soothed by her efforts to stand up for herself, for me even. "She is Voraxian, as Geeri is, and this solar her xanaxana flared in response to me. I have known for many solars now that she is likely my mate, and my beast's, and this solar proved it. Her eyes illuminated in color, and I fully transformed. The cocorangee can attest to it."

I frown as Slascax continues to shake her head. "That is a problem."

"The tribe will understand…"

"Cera! It's a problem because N'gon has *already begun* courting Latanya. Last solar, he openly declared his intentions by kneeling before Latanya and Latanya accepted when she kissed him."

"She did *what*?"

Latanya tenses and her hold on my hand firms as she looks up at me with wide eyes, full of panic. "I…kiss cheek…" She points to her own. "And only because…he says he'll find my parents…"

"And he did, Latanya. He found the tre'or'oro you requested of him."

"What did he find?" Latanya and I say at the same time.

Slascax's face caves, her expression one of mourning. "Latanya, N'gon has found your mother."

Latanya wriggles out of my grip until I'm forced to release her, the blood draining out of my body as soon as her palm leaves mine. I feel as if I could collapse, the beast inside of me roaring with the urge to bury itself beneath the ocean floor, or perhaps tear out N'gon's spine. "He did *what?*"

"He found your mother."

"But he said…he said three solars…It has only…been one."

He said three solars. It has only been one. She gave him the option of seeking tre'or'oro. Any doubt I had at Slascax's first words are undone by Latanya's last ones. I force myself to freeze — not to stagger — as Latanya walks away from me. *She kissed him. She gave him her tre'or'oro request. She betrayed me.*

Cera. Cera… *I told her nothing of the mating rituals, only that they existed. If N'gon discovered them…* I muffle a roar behind my hand, rage at N'gon for his cunning and rage at myself for my hubris. I had assumed that no other would attempt to court Latanya while she remained a deliha — it is not done on Revatu, therefore I had not felt the need to explain the rituals to Latanya. But N'gon must have discovered them…and he had no such qualms about courting her before her deliha training was complete.

And she accepted. And now I have no idea how to proceed — not without violence.

Slascax grimaces as she speaks. "Come quickly. She is injured."

Latanya's hands clasp over her mouth and her knees tremble. I can sense she's about to fall instants before she starts to and I quickly step to her side and catch her. Whatever happens between me and her and N'gon is now irrelevant. "Come, Latanya, we need to get to the healer."

She looks up at me, fear in her gaze that I raxing *hate*, but when she nods again I understand that whatever happened between her and N'gon doesn't matter. She trusts *me*. And I will not let her down.

Not like I have already.

We race across Revatu, me scooping her up to carry her at a point when she trips over a nasty root. Latanya is shaking by the time we approach the open door to the healer's hut, located just off of the convening square. It is one of the only structures on Revatu that is on the ground and, as a result, is well fortified and guarded.

The guards stare at us and though it takes some time, they eventually scent what has transpired and their expressions turn surprised and disproving — to me — while remaining empathetic — to her. As it should be. I am pleased by their response and offer them short nods. They are content to glare.

Latanya slips inside and I follow, sticking close to the wall so as to make space for her and the healers. The sight inside surprises me first, before it alarms.

Latanya had described her mother to me, but I've never met a Lemoran before. I hadn't been able to picture it. In my mind, I'd pictured a creature as delicate and soft as Latanya and N'gon are, but the Lemoran female sprawled across the emergency cot has rough, mottled brown skin, no hair at all, and shocking, white twin horns. One of them is chipped — broken — nearly in half. Latanya gasps and goes to her, her hands fluttering in small gestures towards her mother's broken horn, as if she's more concerned for it than the large hole above her mother's hip — which is the cause for my alarm.

The healers don't acknowledge Latanya and I move forward, grabbing Latanya's shoulders and pulling her out of their way as they swarm the injured female. She's out cold. Latanya's shaking.

"How…what…"

"Is there a status, Memorna?" I ask the lead healer. She looks up from across the female's body, her expression tight.

"The wound is deep. It doesn't look good."

Latanya makes a small squeaking sound, like she's trying to hold in a sob. I wrap my arms around her shoulders and pull her into my chest, hoping that this is…okay as a means of providing comfort. When she reaches up and squeezes my forearm, I know that it is.

"And what will you be able to do for her, healer?"

She shoots me an annoyed look. "Heal her," she mutters sardonically, the wisecracker she is. "That is my title, isn't it?"

"You…can fix her?"

Her tone softens as she turns her attention to Latanya in my grip. "Shenti, and without interruption, a lot faster, though your *friend*, Neg'orn, did not seem so confident."

"Careful, Memorna," I hiss.

Memorna glances at me, and then seems to register the scents Latanya and I carry and the way we're standing together. She gawks, then slams her jaw shut and shakes her head slightly. "You will be sent for when she wakes. For now, it's best she stays unconscious. It will help her heal faster."

"Do whatever you can for her. She is the mother of my mate."

Memorna nods a little jerkily then. Her gaze flashes to the door. "If needed, I will use the merillian."

I tense. It is a great honor. The merillian reserves we have are weak. We only procure them from the off-worlders and they only come by once in a rotation, sometimes more and sometimes less, but never predictably. To save Latanya's mother, Memorna may need to use all that we have. I nod deeply then and with cooed words of consolation and promises on our healers' behalf I hope to the high seas they'll be able to keep, I escort Latanya from the building.

"Latanya, are you…" My voice trails off as we reach the perimeter of the convening square where Nevo, Orick, Yrkar, Slascax and Mornar wait. I can see Vevaxcra, Geeri, Yoturo, and Neesa approaching in the distance, but I am more concerned by the sight of another. One other. He stands alone in the center of the empty space, arms crossed over his chest as he glares at Latanya triumphantly.

His gaze switches to mine when I look to his face. He grins to show all of his dazzling teeth as he calls Latanya's name. "Latanya, come to your mate."

A deep growl kicks my vocal cords and I feel an already feral, recently loosed beast thrash beneath my skin. My shoulder jerks and, in my peripheral vision, I see Mornar straighten. A small smile plays at the edge of his mouth when my gaze meets his, but I do not respond to the nod of kinship he offers me now that I have become the only other winged beast of Revatu, just like him. I wonder how he knows. Can he see the colors that warp my gaze? Will he stand beside me when I slit N'gon's throat? I *loathe* this male. And yet…he, too, has claim on my female.

"Oh rax…" Latanya whispers. She spins in my grip, turning to face me. Her face is perfect, a precious creation, which makes the sting of her betrayal cut all the deeper. "Grizz, you…must know I did not know…about mating…" Her words are stuttered and her lips still tremble. "I don't want…to mate…him…"

"Shh…shhh…" I nod, knowing, because I do know. Her betrayal, for that's what it was, was entirely unintentional. I have seen how she reviles him. I have heard her ask for his disembowelment at my hand, with my claws. I know she doesn't want him, regardless of her actions. "I know. I will explain our connection before the tribe…"

"Cera." I freeze, hand suspended mid-air where it had been destined for her cheek. I want to catch her tears, lick them away before they can fall, carry her so that she can rest her full weight and the weight of all of her fears on me. Her mate. Her *Xiveri*. "Negunn has…information about…the others…my father. He will not…give it to me…if I do not…go with him."

"Cera," I bellow, the words coming out on flame that I know Slascax and Orick, standing in the periphery, see. "You do not expect me to be able to let you walk away from me and into another male's arms…least of all one who I have seen, with my own eyes, bring you harm."

Her brow crinkles above her nose. She stiffens and lowers her voice. "I expect you…to trust me."

My beast beats at the underside of my chest. I stare down at her face, lost in her gaze as I wonder how in the setting sun she expects me to be able to do this. "He could harm you…"

"He won't. At least…not until after…"

"Latanya," I hiss.

And then she does the damnable. She steps away from me. She holds my gaze and pitches her voice loudly

— loud enough for N'gon, and the rest of the tribe, to hear. "Thank you, Negunn. I will go…with you now…to find my tre'or'oro if it's true that you have…found where my father and the others…are." As she speaks to N'gon, my claws cut into my palms and my spirit sinks lower and lower into the ground, like my wings, so newly discovered, have just been cut.

"I have. Come, Latanya. Come take my hand and I will show you to where I found your *mother*." I notice he speaks the final word with a disdain so apparent it appears even through his translator.

Latanya winces and clenches her teeth and I watch as the others stare between the two of us as if expecting something…like me to kill N'gon. And I might have, had Latanya not turned back to me and hissed, "Trust me… and follow close. Something…is wrong… I feel it." She touches the center of her chest where I feel a presence that was not there the solar before. Hers. Occupying too much space, wanting too much of me to keep my feet rooted, even for the next few moments it takes to watch her disappear on N'gon's arm into the forest.

I'm still standing there, counting the seconds before I can launch myself after them without being tracked. I need a few more. Just a few more. At my side, Mornar says, "She has chosen you. I can see it, even if she goes with him now. He has something she needs. Once she takes it, she will come back…"

"*If* she *can* come back. N'gon is a wily, cunning male. I've underestimated him too many times to count."

Mornar grimaces. Geeri comes to his side and slides her hand over his shoulder. "Don't make the mistake of underestimating *her*, though."

My chest pulses. I nod at Geeri, understanding her words for what they are. My tribe members — beings I've known since my memory begins — stand behind the pair. All of them look worried. All of them will stand beside me when I go after them.

"You may not have courted her correctly, but I've seen how she looks at you," Slascax says. "And perhaps more importantly, how she looks at N'gon."

Nevo crosses her arms over her chest and nods in agreement. Only Geeri continues to frown. "You shouldn't have asked to be her dulaha."

"I know that. Don't you think I know that?" I round on her.

Mornar steps forward. "Watch yourself, my Hunger knows its form better than yours does." He challenges me, but I'm not sure right now it matters. I'm seething and struggle to take several deep breaths that do absolutely nothing to calm me. Yrkar comes to my side and pushes me back a step. I allow him to force my retreat.

"She is my Xiveri mate. She is Voraxian," I tell Geeri.

"She has no ridges," Geeri says with a frown, gesturing to the raised bumps above her eyes. They illuminate white now, a color I know to mean surprise, followed by a darker fuchsia which usually relates to her confusion.

"The coloring did not appear in her skin, but in her eyes. She glowed every color, as you do for Mornar sometimes."

Her ridges flare then, turning the dark blue skin of her forehead to a wildly bright light. She frowns more deeply. "I've never seen a hybrid like her before…"

"That I cannot help. But, for now, I've waited long enough…"

Orick steps in front of me, forming a wall with Slascax and Vevaxcra and Yoturo. "It hasn't been long enough. N'gon will see us coming."

"It's likely he'll withhold information on the whereabouts of her kin if he does," Nevo adds. "He's a slippery bastard."

I huff, tasting char. "I *cannot* wait for him to savage her."

"Trust her," Geeri says, "just as she asks. Just give her a little more time."

"I trust her. It's *him* I don't trust."

"Then, at the very least, trust that she is of his planet. She knows his mind better than you do and if she took her First Leap in order to stay away from him, just as you and the hunters who found her first say she did, then trust that she knows how to evade him and stay alive."

I rub my face roughly, my beast seeming to understand Geeri's words better than I do because he settles, at least enough to keep me from breathing fire. I pace and glance periodically up at the sun, watching it move so raxing slowly.

"How deep did he travel when he found Latanya's mother, Nevo?"

"I'm not sure." She shakes her head.

I stop pacing. "What? You were assigned to guard the reevi farmers this solar. You should have been tracking his movements."

"He disappeared at a point," Orick adds, coming to her defense. "We weren't with him when he found Latanya's mother. He reconvened at the edge of the divide carrying her and asking for our help to transport her back."

Something sour and sticky slicks across my chest. "And how did he say the female was injured?"

Nevo grimaces, her teeth clenching together and her lips feathering around her tusks. "He doesn't know. He claims to have found her like that."

"Grizz!" I'm about to take off in a sprint when the sound of Memorna's voice holds me back. I turn and see the female standing in the doorway of the healing hut. She gestures at me wildly. "She's awake. She's asking for Latanya."

I turn, hesitating, but only for a moment. In the healing hut, I blink quickly so that my eyes may better adjust to the dimmer light. When they do, I see the Lemoran female attempting to sit up on the cot. The healers are holding her down, but she's fighting. A ferocious one. I see where Latanya gets it.

"Latanya?" Her lips curl and she shakes her head.

"Cera, I'm not Latanya," I tell her, hoping that her translator works as Latanya's does. "I'm Grizz," I say, feeling rather silly as this is not my born name, but the one I feel born into as it's the one Latanya gave me. "I am Latanya's mate. Her Xiveri."

"Xiveri," the female repeats. She says words in her tongue that I don't understand, but I hear Latanya's name again, followed closely by N'gon's.

"N'gon claims her as a mate. He tricked her into accepting his hand, using the location of your mate and the others of your kind as bait. They are going to retrieve them now. I intend to follow."

Her eyes grow large and her hand surges forward, reaching across her body to point to her wound. The action pains her and her entire expression twists. The healers admonish her and attempt to push her back into a fully reclined position — this time succeeding — but not before she says, "Negunn." Her hand stretches up and clasps at the hilt of an imaginary blade, one that she stabs herself with. Her eyes open. She meets my gaze. *"Negunn."*

I throw myself from the healer's hut before it is too late, because my beast does not hesitate. I transform in the center of the square, wind rushing off of my wings as they unfurl. I take flight right there and go after my mate and the one who covets her. The one I promised her I'd disembowel.

13

Latanya

I feel sticky sweat along my spine that's only half to do with the humidity of the mainland, which is several degrees hotter than it is on the Hunger-free Revatu. The rest has to do with the fact that Negunn's walking behind me where I can't see him unless I turn all the way around.

"Are we almost there?" I ask nervously. Asking Grizz to trust me was a lot when I barely trust myself with Negunn. He always outsmarts me. *Always.* And I don't know what he has planned, but this isn't this straight forward — it *can't* be. Negunn knows *me* well enough to know by now that I won't just have sex with him for leading me to my father and I sure as comets won't mate him for life because of it. What is he thinking? What is he planning? What has he already done?

"Something's different about you," Negunn says instead of answering me.

I glance at him over my shoulder to see him watching me with a frown. He isn't even looking at my ass either. Hmm… That really can't be good. "I'm worried. My mom is dying."

"The wound is deep. You should prepare yourself." He nods solemnly at me, but there's a flatness to his gaze that makes me think that he isn't so apologetic at all.

A creeping feeling claims the back of my skull and makes my spine arch. "How was she injured?"

"I didn't...I don't know, Latanya. I found her near to where the beacon told me the others would be." He pulls the beacon out of his hide vest. It's a broken piece of something. I don't know where he got it, or how he could have. All of the pods were dissolved in the Hunger solars ago...

Unless he's had it all along.

My voice is lower and angrier when I speak next. "You're an intelligent male. What do you *think* caused it?"

"Likely one of this feral place's more feral beasts." He tips his head forward and gestures at a glowing light on the flat panel in his hand. "Just through these trees. Here, let me lead." He steps past me and I let him — I can't see any reason it would be a bad idea to have him at my front, rather than at my back.

Just as his shoulder brushes my chest, he pauses and leans in to my neck. He inhales deeply. "You smell off."

"I haven't bathed in a few solars," I lie.

His eyes narrow. "Then why is your hair wet?" He picks up a lock of my hair and lets it fall.

I shrug. "It's humid."

He snorts, glaring between my eyes. "I can see a red sheen flickering in your eyes. What is it? You sick? Whatever it is, I don't want to catch it."

I snort. "You won't, I'm sure." I blink, hoping to control my emotions better than this. I've never shined with any sort of emotion before. *Maybe Grizz was right, maybe I am Voraxian, in part at least.*

"It's getting brighter. And there's black, too."

So much for control… "I don't know, Negunn. I can't feel it or see it, myself. It must be this place." I don't know what the colors correspond to, either. I'll have to ask Geeri. All I know is what I *feel*. And what I feel is hate.

"Well, don't let it turn you into a beast, like them, Latanya. I don't want a filthy beast for a mate."

I hold my tongue and let him stomp off. "You won't have me for a mate at all," I whisper under my breath.

Negunn moves deftly through a dense layer of bushes with leaves the size of my body and thorns the size of my face, while I take a few cuts and scrapes to my forearms, one of them kind of deep. I hiss as I come through the thickets and I'm so distracted by my own pain that I don't immediately notice what lies directly before me.

And then I hear my name.

"Latanya!"

"You found her…"

"Has anyone seen Nesha or Prenatio?"

"Someone find her parents!"

My people. *All* of the delegates of Quadrant One. All forty of them, or nearly at least, all rainbow-colored hair and golden faces. All except for one other outsider — a Hypha, with small black eyes, orange skin and fins protruding from the sides of his face. They come forward, crowding around me until I'm inundated and Negunn, of all foul creatures, has to save me.

"Hey, hey, give her some space. She's spent the past dozen solars with these beasts. She's shaken, understandably."

So many Quadrant One princes and princesses and merchants and traders and skilled professionals nod at me solemnly, a pity in their eyes I haven't ever seen. Cera, they may pity me for the way I look to them, but they've never pitied me like they care about me. Like they're worried. Not like they are now.

Wait. What did Negunn say?

"Wait. What?"

Negunn grips my shoulders, looping one strong arm around my back. He nods at all of the Quadrant One faces and says sadly, "They've brainwashed her into thinking she's one of them. You can expect that she won't take it lightly when we attack."

"What!" I pull back, putting space between us. I open my mouth, aware that my first instinct is to shout and rant but I'm so used to speaking in stilted Revatu that, for once, the words don't come that fast.

They get trapped behind my teeth and, when I go to say them, they come out measured and slow. "Wait. You plan…to attack the Revatu?"

Negunn glowers at me, but it's another member of the community that answers. "Negunn has told us of their barbaric ways. He says that attack is our only chance of survival."

"We have the weapons to do it," a male I think is called Trenno says, holding up a blaster. "Well, we have some weapons."

"And Negunn says they have none. That they're barbarians with no access to technology."

I open my mouth and I don't say anything, not for the first instant. Because in the second, I know what I need to do. "Negunn is right." I look out across the crowd, bewildered by their numbers and impressed that they've survived so long. But not in a good state. The longer I look, the longer I realize that they are injured, almost all of them. Clothes singed black, some nursing wounds and burns. One delegate has a swollen cheek and another two lie flat on their backs beneath thin gold blankets retrieved from the pods. They're alive, but they've been suffering for solars now when they didn't have to...

What is Negunn's goal here?

I turn to look at the foul wretch, the expression on his face murderous. "Careful, Latanya. They know already how you love the beasts..."

"I don't love the beasts," *I love* one *beast*, "but I know more about them than you do. And I know that our weapons will do nothing against them, not when some of them can transform into armored *dragons* that can fly."

That causes a stir, panic setting in as the gathered beings look down at what they've put together to launch their assault. I note that there are only three blasters I can see, while the rest of the weapons look crudely cobbled together — spears and sticks carved of reevi shoots, pieces of golden steel from the disintegrated pods tied together with vines and bits of fabric... I frown. Negunn works with the shoots and didn't even tell our own people that he could use the innards as twine? And he plans to lead a revolt with them?

"You cannot lead a revolt with this."

"She lies," Negunn shouts, pitching his voice loudly, full of authority that cannot be denied. "You can't trust her. She's been corrupted by them."

I open my mouth to rebut this, but Trenno himself answers, "Why would she lie about our chances?"

"And dragons?" An older female shouts. Her name is Opo and I know her. She's from my home town and has always been kind to my family. "That is a rather outlandish lie, don't you think?"

I nod at her, meeting her gaze. "Opo, have you seen my father? Why is he absent? And does anyone know why my mother was so badly injured?"

"Injured?" Opo hisses. She comes forward, approaching me, though her stare remains trained on Negunn. "I thought they went with you, Negunn, to look for Latanya." Opo touches my back, but I realize that she's trying to pull me away from him.

Negunn must notice it, too, because his stare hardens. "I lost them when the molten rock came."

"You *didn't*. You found my mother."

"A lie," Negunn barks out a laugh. "How would you even know? You were with your beastly friends."

"I know because you brought her to the healers of Revatu."

"Lies."

"And she's fine. They *do* have technology. They have merillian and they'll be able to heal her. They'll be able to heal all of you. There's no reason for you to live in such desperation."

"Lies!" Negunn's shout is triumphant as he points at my face. "I told you she sides with them."

"Why would she?" Opo shouts. "And what happened to her parents? Where are Nesha and Prenatio?"

Negunn's face has started to turn a deep, deep shade of gold, almost copper. I step away from him and I wonder if many of the others notice that they have, too. "They're likely lost. They don't know the wilderness like I do, but they haven't been lost long. I'm sure they'll be back soon."

"Negunn, what did you do?" Panic claws at my throat. "Where is my father?"

Voices all start speaking at once, clamoring until none can be heard. I approach Negunn, wanting answers with a desperation that borders on insanity. I push him in the center of the chest while his attention is turned to someone else, shouting far less important questions as far as I'm concerned.

He turns to me, his hand whipping out on instinct and, on instinct, I duck. But instead of hitting me, he hits another male standing behind me. The weaker male staggers back and falls onto his ass.

"Negunn!" Opo shouts. "What are you doing?"

He looks frazzled in a way he never does, hair shooting up as he runs an evidently sweaty hand through it. "Trying to calm you all down. We're being ripped apart by the words of an alien who's been brainwashed by monsters!"

"They aren't monsters, Negunn! You are! Did you hurt my mom?" I shove him again and he staggers back into a tree. One of the spikes nicks him and he hisses, his shoulder coming back bloody. "Did you?"

I move to shove him again, this time grabbing him by the edges of his vest. He grabs my wrists so hard I know he could break them if he wanted but right now I don't care. I whisper, "If you hurt my mom, I will have Grizz gut you like he promised he would."

"That monster can't touch me."

"He's my *mate*, Negunn, and shenti, he is a monster. He bred me as one." I dodge the first blow, but not the second. The back of Negunn's hand hits me across the face hard enough I go flying. The thud of landing on my back is second to the sting in my cheek as I lie there, staring up at the clouds, listening to sounds of outrage and dissent. I'm not sure any of them have seen Negunn before — really seen him — he's so good at cloaking himself under lies and arrogance.

But Revatu does something to us all, doesn't it? It shows us who we're meant to be, who we truly are beneath layers of gold glitter and feigned bravado.

I smile as a shadow passes across the sun. A moment later, I feel the breeze. Like two sails of some great ship moving in perfect synchronicity, the wings of my mate's megalithic form beat and the pressure in my chest settles.

"Grizz," I whisper, pointing up. "My mate! Lower your weapons!"

"Fire!" Negunn screams.

I lurch up and see that half of the group has turned their attention — and what weak weapons they have — up towards the blinding sun. Staggering into Trenno's side, I grip his arm and yank his blaster down. "Don't! He won't harm any of you." Well, Negunn doesn't count.

"Fire, you fools! He's coming to kill all of you!"

"He can breathe fire! If he were intending to kill you, he'd have done so by now!" I shout back and it is apparently the wrong thing to say or, perhaps, badly timed because Grizz chooses that moment to release a great ball of fire into the sky as he spirals down, down, down.

A blast blazes up into the air, not Trenno's but belonging to someone else in the crowd. It leaves scorch marks across Grizz's underbelly, marring its perfection. "Cera!" I shriek. The blaster fires again, this time causing Grizz to jerk back up. The wind his wings creates is enough to swirl my hair around my face. I hear several others cry out and behind me, Opo falls over.

"Grizz…lift up! You're scaring…everyone!" The beast sweeps its gaze across the crowd, the enormous eye settling on me, but only briefly, before the entire winged thing lifts another length up into the air, away from us.

"It listened to her," someone shouts. "It listened to Latanya!"

"Kill it!" Negunn roars.

"Don't!" But this shout isn't mine, but a voice that is wholly familiar to me.

My heart catches. My mouth opens. I turn. I see everyone has turned with me. We stare towards the trees where a hobbling creature emerges, one that I recognize, but only faintly, because I've never seen him so weakened before.

"Dad!" I scream, charging forward, but the crowd is thick.

My dad looks down from the treeline where he staggers into the clearing. He's clutching one of his arms to his chest. It looks badly mangled. He points the other one towards us. "Do not trust Negunn. He has deceived us! He tried to kill me. Nesha intervened." He coughs, nearly doubling over, his thick, pale pink beard matted with bright gold blood that terrifies me. "Where did you take her, you monster?"

"Dad! Mom's okay," I shout, surging forward away from the group, and I watch his eyes fall to me and fill with light.

"Latanya? We've been searching for you..."

"I'm fine." I stagger up the short incline and try to catch him but, even though he isn't a huge male, I'm still too weak to support him fully. "Dad, what did he do to you?"

"He stabbed me," my father hisses, looking down at his arm. "He tried to stab me in the heart. I fell...fell over the edge of a cliff. He thought I was dead but I managed to catch onto some sort of clear vine." Clear vine? Or a web? I shudder at what could have happened, grateful that it didn't. "Your mother...she must have followed us. I don't want to imagine what he did to her. But you say...she's alright?" He's breathing hard, wheezing now.

I nod vigorously while, behind me, Negunn keeps shouting orders to kill the beast. "Cera! Don't listen to Negunn. He's mad!" I shout back. "He tried to kill my parents!"

"*That's* madness!" Negunn roars. The crowd starts to split, so I can see him once more. "Why would I try to kill them?"

I open my mouth, but that I don't know.

"*I* know." My father licks his lips, his eyes slinking shut as his face twists in pain. He leans even more of his weight onto me and I shake with the effort it takes to keep him upright."Negunn never wanted to be a prince. He wanted to be a *king*. By learning everything he could from the native community and then convincing us to kill them, he could be." My father coughs and it's the only thing that breaks the short, painful silence.

I don't know what to say. I don't know what to think. My mouth hangs wide open and my heart beats hard and heavy and with a calm that can't belong to me because I have no right to it, with my mom dying and my father following her. I'm still looking at Negunn when his stare finally turns to me, as if *I'm* the reason our people are suddenly staring at him in shock and horror.

I see what he'll do instants before he does it. "Cera, Negunn! Don't!"

But it's too late. He lunges for Trenno's blaster, stealing it from his limp hand, and charges forward. He points it at my dad, who grabs my arm and tries to hold me back, because I realize that I've moved to intercept it — whatever happens next. The blaster fires with one light squeak. A flash of light flares and I close my eyes, bracing for impact, while my father calls my name desperately behind me.

And then comes the thunder. It shakes the ground, knocking me onto my ass. I fall and the blast...doesn't land. I'm covered in shadow that smells like smoke and relief and the Hunger itself. I exhale and look up in time to see a dragon looking down at me.

I smile, "Thank you." And then panic sets in. "Grizz, are you okay?"

The dragon bows its massive head and I realize as it lowers one wing to the ground that he means for me to mount him. I nod. "Where...where's Negunn?"

The wing lifts just slightly and I see Negunn crushed beneath the claw of his back foot. His golden arms are moving though — thrashing really — so I know he can't be too badly hurt. I'm just glad he no longer has hold of his blaster.

"He doesn't deserve to live," I tell Grizz with a frown. The dragon huffs out smoke. I wonder what that means, but I don't question it.

I trust him.

It takes me some time to convince my people to climb onto Grizz's back. It's scary. I pretend I've done this before, but that's a lie and, as we lift up into the sky in large lurches, I worry for all of them. I fly below, not on Grizz's back, but how I spent my mid-solar — clutched in his front claw. My father flies in his other front claw while Negunn continues to thrash in the claw of his back left foot. I smile, wondering what the Revatu will do to him when we return from the mainland. I picture a whole host of tortures I know they're too kind to inflict. But I'm not left long to wonder…

Halfway across the divide, heading back to Revatu from the mainland, I hear a scream. My head whips back and my gaze snags on Negunn's golden form just as Grizz's back claw releases him. Negunn tries to grab for purchase, but as he tumbles out of Grizz's clutches, one massive, sharpened red claw slices across Negunn's stomach.

Intestines, all slippery and liquid gold, spill out in a rush.

Negunn watches them career towards the vines, and then below them towards the web. Negunn looks up and meets my gaze and we're staring at one another as Negunn falls. I wave goodbye to him, satisfied that he'll make a wonderful sacrifice to the cocorangee. And that he's been disemboweled.

And that Grizz kept his promise, after all.

14

Grizz

I spend the late solar with Latanya's parents, as I have for the past five. This solar, Latanya does not join me. At her parents' and my insistence, she's finally gone home — back to *our* home — to sleep, something she hasn't done since she and I were mated, her kin was found, and I finally lived up to the first vow I made her — to disembowel Negunn with my own claws.

"You should...tell Latanya...about the off-worlders, Grizz," her mother, Nesha, tells me through the use of her translator as I reach the doorway. "She will...want to stay...with her...mate. I did."

Her gaze flashes to the male in the cot across the room from her, a male who gave up the last of the merillian reserves the healers intended to use for him in order to heal the burns of one of his fellow shipwrecked friends. It was an honorable decision, one that reserved him the right to decline the First Leap. He declined such a declination, vowing that he would do it once his arm, which had been partially flayed after being caught in the cocorangee web that saved his life, was fully healed.

His actions do not surprise me. Nor do the actions of Latanya's mother — intervening to save her mate's life at the expense of her own and getting herself stabbed by

Negunn in the process. It makes it impossible to believe that Latanya could have ever come from other parents. Cera, she is *of* these creatures, regardless of her provenance or her color, just as she is *of* Revatu, regardless of which star system claims her.

"I will." I nod to them. "Thank you." I start to leave, but hesitate. "If…if she were to make such a choice, would you remain with her here?"

The pair exchange a look, all smiles that suggest they have been in love for a mere moment. Young lovers, so new and green, rather than mated for two long lifetimes. "There is nowhere…we would rather…be…than at our daughter's…side," her father, Prenatio, answers, pain and lethargy competing in his expression as he fights to stay awake. "You chose well…and so…did she…"

I attempt to cage my response, which is a grin as wide as the room. "I have done nothing yet to deserve such an honor, but I vow to make you welcome here and to treat your daughter with all the respect of a goddess." Because that's what she is to me.

"You…did. You finally…got rid of that…rotten egg," Nesha sneers.

"Took long…enough," Prenatio confirms. "We've been trying…to get rid of that…creep for rotations."

I break then and bark out a laugh that startles the healer toiling in the back of the hut with another of the wounded. She breaks her concentration long enough to shoot me a scowl, which I return with a grin as I tell Nesha and Prenatio, "It's a sentiment I understand. I vowed to Latanya I'd kill him the first solar I knew him."

I leave them chuckling at thoughts of murder as I make my way across the convening square. Here, so many new faces mingle with the beings of Revatu, each attempting to train a new deliha. It is…a slow process. We've never had so many off-worlders land at one time. We don't know how many will choose to stay, once they're informed of the possibility of leaving. We also know that only a few *can* leave each rotation given the transportation device the off-worlders usually use.

Latanya, however, would have the first place were she to choose to go. I just hope I can do enough to ensure she won't. Though if she does she must know…she has to know…I'd follow her across the Quadrants.

I return to my home, careful to be quiet as I enter the bedroom and see Latanya sprawled across the bed. I attempt to ignore my sudden growl, because it's the rattling of a beast in a cage. To distract myself, I light a candle…and then I light a few more. Standing back at the foot of the bed, I look down at her.

Her skin shimmers, appearing as a Fata Morgana might to a sun-drunk traveler wandering the deserts alone.

I am such a traveler.

And I am thirsty.

I prowl to the foot of the bed and lift the edge of the ridiculous blanket she insists on using even though here on Revatu it is never cold, and I slide beneath it, appreciating its utility for her scent seems amplified here. It surrounds me and I inhale and inhale and inhale.

She's sleeping on her side and, when I roll her onto her back, doesn't wake. I spread her legs and slide my shoulders between them, moving up to the juncture of her thighs where I press my tusks onto her mound so that it bulges between them, ripe and ready to be devoured. After the solars of stress she's had, I know she needs this.

Or maybe I just need this.

I taste her sweet lips and a moan racks my entire body. Then I slide my tongue inside of her as deep as anatomy will allow. And then a little more as my beast shifts to use his tongue, rather than my own, and spears her a little deeper. I drink. I drink and drink and drink until I'm able to sate my thirst on the orgasm that trembles through her. She makes this terrible, gasping sound and it is only terrible because it ensures that I'm too hard and tense and desperate not to do terrible things to her body in order for her to make that sound for me again.

And again.

Until we're old and grey and can no longer climb. She will need to take me even then because not having her will not be an option. I have a sudden thought that perhaps I am not so different from the deceased N'gon after all…and then I dismiss it, remembering that there is one critical difference between him and me.

When you ask…I say shenti. That's what Latanya told me once and I will never forget it. Maybe it's because *I* asked that she said yes at all. Perhaps if another had, this would have all worked out so very differently and I would be left thirsty, wandering that desert alone.

But I don't think so. I know her light calls to me, just as my flame calls to her. Together, they are bound, just as we are. Xiveri mates, a love that is as eternal as Revatu's ceaseless Thirst and endless Hunger.

I crawl up her body as its tremors subside and I pull the blanket down to my shoulders. She's not fully awake yet, panting and smiling in her sleep as her head turns slowly from one side to the other. I grin. She's so exhausted, I'm sure she could sleep through an explosion. Perhaps I'll need to test that.

I press my knees into the mattress and line myself up with her hot, wet entrance. I lower down onto her and take her right breast roughly in one hand. It's so large my single hand can hardly contain it, but that's why the good creator saw fit to grant me a second hand…

And a mouth.

I pull her nipple into my heat, kneading the flesh around it with my tusks, while below, I press firmly inside of her, keeping my thrusts even and slow as I wait for her to wake fully. I want her attention. I crave it, always.

"Grizz," she moans. "I thought I must…sleep…" she says breathily, a smile on her lips. I know she's been awake this whole time, the little temptress. I love this game. And I love that she loves to play it.

I chuckle. "You would…deny…your mate…" I speak on each thrust, "release?"

"Oh my…rax!" She curses in her own tongue, her head thrown back, her sleepy gaze locked to mine. "Cera…never…"

"Good little goddess…" I kiss her, shoving my tongue in her mouth, because I want to taste everything, but she breaks it.

"I thought I was a good…little monster…" She smiles.

I feel a tittering across my chest, like thousands of small hearts all beating at the same time, perhaps the connection of a thousand Xiveri that have come before us, telling me that this one in particular is all mine.

I settle between her thighs, taking a moment to simply look down at her. I kiss her in the center of her forehead. "I love you, Latanya."

Her eyes flutter and muscles in her neck strain. She gasps. "You…you do?"

I pick up my pace, a sudden fever gripping me as I acknowledge what I've been wanting to say to her for some time. "Shenti."

Her core squeezes my length and sweat climbs down my shoulder blades to cover my back in dew as she tests my restraint. And then she breaks it entirely. "Good, because I love you, too."

"Augh! Latanya, you don't know what you do to me." I wrench out of her on a moan — our shared one — flip her over and drag the wetness from her pussy up to her tighter rear hole.

"You won't fit there," she says desperately while I shove two pillows underneath her hips. "I promise you won't fit there, Grizz."

She's right. I know she is. But what I want from her here is more important than that tight, tantalizing hole. I arch over her body, smothering her down onto the bed. She can't escape. Not with my size. Not in her submissive position. Not with my hand around her neck. Not when she has just challenged what I wanted most from her.

What she has already given me.

What I already own.

"Trust me," I whisper against her cheek. "Do you trust me?"

Her eyes meet mine and they're glossy and star-glazed. She looks so lovely. So raxing lovely. "*Always*," she answers and I smirk at her strange language. She smiles at me in return. "Shenti," she repeats.

I kiss the tip of her nose. "Good."

And then I slide inside — not a lot, just the tip, and that's where I keep it. To torture us both. I just want to milk myself inside of her tightest hole, fill it up, watch it spill over like the Mouth of the mainland mountain. My barbs inflate and deflate in small pulses as I torture myself, knowing I would never risk tearing her, or hurting her, knowing that I could never latch there. But I idle there, for the sick fun of it, and microthrust into her back hole, stretching it with the bloated head of my cock.

My hand snakes beneath her body and moves over her clit roughly. "Does it feel good?" I say, while I idle on the crossroads of agony and bliss.

"Rax…" She moans. "I'm going to come."

"Good little monster. But *only* on my command," I hiss.

"I can't…stop…" She barks instants before her body shudders and she spills hot liquid all over my hand, coming without my permission. Naughty, bratty little monster that she is. This is deserving of punishment, so I edge inside of her just a little bit further. She bites out a moan and streaks of discomfort appear on her face, but I take her to this edge and this is where I keep her.

"Naughty little monster. You will need to be punished for your insolence."

"Augh," she moans, head thrown back. My hand comes around her neck and I squeeze as the beast growls in my chest. Tension shoots up the backs of my legs and I stiffen, fighting the urge to impale her, but I keep fighting against my beast's wants as well as my own as sensations too pleasurable to put names to cover my entire body and wrap themselves around my steeled form.

"Latanya," I heave, sounding like a desperate man. Sounding like that traveler who has found that oasis and glutted himself on its offering. "Tell me again. Once more."

She smiles and whispers against the sex-stained sheets, "I love…you…Grizz…"

"Augh!" The head of my cock still wedged in her body, I can't restrain myself any longer. I release into her, pouring milky cum into her body, stretching her tightest hole to accommodate the pale green desire that claims her.

"Grizz," she moans. And as she turns her head and blinks over her shoulder at me languidly, I see the galaxy in her eyes and I feel the rich tangy burn in the back of my throat reminding me of the enemies I have vanquished for her and will vanquish again.

I push the hair out of her face as I pull up, flip her body over and bury myself in her pussy where my barbs are finally able to release. I heave a sigh, satisfied then, as we lock together tight, unable to part. Keeping her pinned as she is, I lift my hand and smack the outside of her hip and ass.

She jerks, surprise lighting her face and her eyes in a bright sheen which spills color over her cheeks. White — her surprise — blue — her satisfaction — and purple — her lust for me. "What was…that for?"

"Did I give you permission to come?" I snarl, loving the way her stare hooks on my tusks, pupils expanding, color brightening.

She bites her lush bottom lip but doesn't reply.

"Not answering won't save you."

She huffs, the little brat. I grin, adoring her rebelliousness. Gives me a thousand and one reasons to punish her in a thousand and one positions. "Cera."

I swat her rear again, smoothing my hand over the heat my palm leaves behind. "Ouw!"

"That didn't hurt. But this next one will if you disobey me again." I start to sit up, kneeling as my barbs make it possible for me to thrust once more. I lift her knees to her shoulders and she yelps.

"Grizz…" There's something in her tone that brokers a pause from me.

"Shenti?"

"We…haven't talked…about kits…"

"Cera, we haven't."

"I have a…an implant, for now. To keep me from… having kits. But I could…" She bites her bottom lip, flicks her gaze up to mine. It glows in a whole history of colors, a history I don't know, but that I want to. For now, I merely allow the sensation of rightness to fill me as she looks at me with adulation and wonder and nervousness. This is all so new. The most wondrous adventure. "I could take it out."

Pride fills my chest and I smolder. My dragon exalts. I want to say *shenti* to her and remove it now, watch her stomach bloat, first with our cum and then with our kitlings, but… "We need time. Much has happened. And I would not mind having you to myself a little longer. I already am forced to share you with my beast, and I don't know if I need to remind you that I'm a savage, jealous creature."

I lower onto her body, hooking her knees over my shoulders as I move. Her eyelids flutter and a smile breaks out over her face. "Shenti…but I don't…want to wait…too long," she says between gasps. "I…feel an urge…with you."

"I feel it, too. But there is much we have to explore together and all the time in the worlds to do it. There is…" I pause, starting to slow. "There is also something I need to tell you…"

"About what?"

The cruel male that I am, I pound into her once with force, as if hoping to distract her. *That's exactly what I'm doing.* "There is a way for you to leave…to return to your home world, if you want."

She smiles and thrusts her rear back onto my cock, making my throat contract. I release an unattractive gurgle. She laughs, "Cera, there isn't."

"Cera?"

"Because if I did…how could I leave my heart… behind me?"

I grab a fistful of her hair, overcome as I draw close to her, close enough to count her eyelashes. I kiss the tops of her eyelids, the top of her nose. "You know I would go with you."

"But I am home. Isn't that…what you told me once?"

"Latanya," I whisper, thrusting into her again and again. I bring her near an orgasm but hold back, just long enough to whisper, "Tell me again…"

"Sesiva…a?"

"You know what…" I draw the words out while a grin spreads slowly, slyly over her face.

"My…Revatu…not so good. I think…I may need…to hear the words…from you, first…"

"*I love you.*" I pound into her roughly then, just as roughly as our first mating. I show her no quarter as fire claws up my throat and my cock, buried deep inside of her body, begins to expand to the beast's size. We both look down at her stomach, able to see its outline. Her pupils dilate, her gasps coming hotter. I know she loves it — and me — and I grin. "And little monster that you are, after this, you will not forget again."

One rotation later…

15

Latanya

Hands on my body are how I wake most solars — strong, sensual strokes, subtle kisses, undressing me, redressing me, or even fitting me for new clothes — but not like this.

"Latanya." He shakes my shoulder.

"Hmmph." I shrug my shoulder back, trying to dislodge him, but he's a persistent brute.

"Latanya, they're here."

"Who?"

He pauses, "The off-worlders."

I flip onto my back, suddenly feeling more awake. I rub a hand down my face and try to focus on his, but the light is so dim, filtering in white through the open curtains. It must be very early. I smile. "Really?"

He nods, though he doesn't smile in response. In fact, his eyes look…a little tortured. My smile grows and I stroke my fingers down the side of his face. "You're a dragon, remember. Don't be scared. They can't beat you up."

He snorts, some of the fear draining from his expression. "Cheeky monster."

"Though, you know, I have heard that the shifters of Sasor might just be able to. If you're naughty, I'll tell the off-worlders to drop you off there."

He grabs the pillow from beneath my head and yanks it out from under me. He grabs the blanket next and fans it down to reveal my fully unclothed body. "Ouw!" I yelp, cool air sticking to my skin unapologetically. I jolt up and throw one of the remaining pillows at him. "Brute!"

"Beast," he corrects with a wink. "And there are *no* other beasts that could defeat mine. Not here, not on Sasor, not anywhere."

"Cocky brute."

"*Beast*. In fact, I'm certain the only thing that can defeat me is a little monster named Latanya."

I stick my tongue out at him as he teases, but get out of bed and dress quickly, excitement rattling through my skin and making me sweat in nervous anticipation. I wonder who they are. From what Grizz described, it sounds like pirates — Niahhorru or perhaps Eshmiri, though I'm pretty sure Eshmiri don't have spikes down their backs or four arms, so I'd be willing to bet on the former. In either case, I haven't had much interaction with Niahhorru pirates before, though from what my parents say, they're ghastly creatures to do business with and are twice as likely to rob you blind as they are to barter with you.

I know I'm not the only curious one either, because the convening square is packed by the time Grizz and I arrive hand-in-hand, hearts beating in sync. I can feel it. I'm so in tune to it now, it's almost creepy. My hearts and his — and his beast's.

Revatu and the shipwrecked from Quadrant One all gather around the periphery to watch the negotiations happen. We already decided as a tribe what we were hoping to get and what we were willing to trade for it. Nevo, Yrkar and Orick conduct the negotiations this time, with Opo assisting to translate since her Meero is better than Geeri's now that she's rotations out of practice.

"Where's the ship?" I ask.

"There is no ship. They use some kind of transportation device that can bring them planetside without having to dock."

I nod, impressed. "Wow."

"You've seen nothing yet. Come. I'd like for them to… to meet you."

Curious at his tone and his suggestion, I cock my head and let Grizz lead me through the crowd. I wasn't so surprised to find that almost *all* of Quadrant One wants to stay, though I was a little surprised to find out why. The ones I asked why said it was because this is a place where they didn't have to worry about climbing the social ladder or attending silly events or trying to attain princedom. There are five that do want to leave and they all agreed that they would miss the ease of living on Revatu, too, but there are beings that they left behind that they just aren't ready to say bye to.

That I understand completely.

The decision would have been a lot harder had my parents wanted to leave. But, as it stands, there's no chance I'd go back to what I left. Here, I have everything I need.

I squeeze Grizz's hand and he looks back at me, offering me a quizzical look and a grin. I open my mouth to tell him something profound I'm sure, or maybe just to call him a beast again, but he steps to the side and I gasp as I take in the sight of the off-worlders for the very first time.

"Oh my stars…"

The female leading the charge is *not* Niahhorru. She does not have grey skin, four arms or spikes growing out of her head, but has long, coiled dark brown hair and skin the *exact* same shade of brown as mine. And her features are just like mine. Just. like. mine! I can't even believe it. The eyes, the nose, the placement of the mouth…she has the same color teeth, all square like mine, no tusks or fangs or fins to speak of, and even though she's rounder than I am, there's no mistaking the similarities between our species. Or that we may be the same species. The only difference between us that I can see is her tongue, which has no ridges, and her eyes that don't expel light when she looks up and sees me for the first time and falls completely silent.

"Holy stars."

She stands in a cluster of Niahhorru pirates — familiar faces — alongside another female who *might* be of the same species she is, but I'm not sure. This one has pale skin and hair the color of flame. It's striking — shocking even. And I'm so focused on her that I don't immediately notice the kits until one points directly at me.

"Look, Mama," it says. And it speaks…I don't know what language it speaks in. It isn't Meero, but it *must* be a known language because my translator is the newest model — was a rotation ago, at least — and I can understand his words.

I look down at the kit and it's clearly a male, but he's...a hybrid combination of the female before me and the Niahhorru pirate behind her. The pirate carries another kit in his arms, this one female and smaller than her male sibling. The female kit has long black hair that falls in ropes in a mohawk down the back of her head where, instead, the male kitling has spikes that resemble smaller versions of the massive tines that stick out of his father's head and rip all the way down his back. And they aren't the only two.

I spy two other hybrid kitlings in the mix, clustered amidst the Niahhorru. The kits have skin that's either grey or brown or sometimes both. Spikes, ropes, or coiled hair like their brown-skinned mother's. They come with Niahhorru features or features like hers, too. And each and every one of them is breathtaking.

I am spellbound.

"Holy *fuck*," the pale-skinned female says in almost the exact same tone as the first. She uses a word that doesn't sift through my translator properly, but that I can tell is definitely a curse. "Is she...human?" she asks the one with skin like mine.

That female shakes her head and takes a few steps forward, favoring her left leg. "Her hair...that hair is Drakesh." She pauses while I absorb what she's just told me. Drakesh? I'm...Drakesh? Not Voraxian, as Geeri and Grizz speculated?

I'm about to ask when the female shrieks, "SHROV! DO YOU KNOW WHAT THIS MEANS?" She charges forward, arms outstretched. I back up into Grizz's chest, which rumbles with the growl he emits. Clearly, his beast doesn't see this female as a threat because he makes no move to intervene as she grabs my shoulders and shakes me as much as her shorter body can. "YOU'RE THE MISSING HYBRID!"

"Whoooooaaaaat?" I wheeze.

She finally stops and lets out a whooping laugh as she looks over her shoulder at the other female staring dumbfounded at me. "She's the missing hybrid. The one we've been looking for. Can you believe it?"

The female shakes her head. "Centare," she answers in Meero, "I really fucking can't. Miari's going to freak."

"Miari?" I ask.

"The queen of Voraxia. You and she are the same species. You're both hybrids. Half-human, half-Drakesh, born out of a terrible Hunt on Voraxia that's since been banned. There were six hybrids born of the first Hunt and so far, we've identified five. Miari's been desperate to find the last. *You* are the last, but you…You…you have to come with us…"

I smile at her, disbelief coloring my gaze in what I know are shades of white surprise and blue satisfaction. I feel Grizz tense at my back, but I reach up and take his hand on my shoulder and give it a gentle squeeze.

"I'd love to hear the story, but on Revatu's soil. *This* is where I belong."

The female's eyes widen as she takes in the beings surrounding me. My family. A surprising surge of tears comes to her eyes and I feel it mirrored in mine succinctly. "Rhork, hand me the yeeyar screen."

I balk as the name clicks into place. Rhork — Rhorkanterannu, the Niahhorru pirate *king*. Holy raxing suns! He's *here?* He's one of the quadrant's most dangerous and elusive beings and I'm meeting him face to face and watching as he's ordered around by a female half his height while he seems perfectly gleeful about it.

He comes forward and slides a blob of black matter into the female's hand. It expands, forming what looks like a holoscreen — advanced yeeyar technology that makes my mind whirl as this is the first I've ever seen it.

The female, clearly adept at such technology, wields it effortlessly while she starts gesturing again with her free hand. "I'll give you twice the amount of merillian y'all asked for if you just let me take your picture, maybe record your image for a few instants." The pirates behind her grumble in discontent, but she just waves them off dismissively and shouts over her shoulder, "Are you insane? I *have* to show Miari and Svera — they're going to shit their pants!"

Turning back to me, she says, "Miari is the queen of Voraxia, but Svera is the ruler of our people." *Our people.* "She rules a small planet in the Voraxian federation called Heimo and they've been worried about you. So worried. They thought they lost you. It would mean the worlds to them to know you're alright. I know it means the worlds to *me*."

My heart squeezes fiercely and Grizz squeezes my shoulders at the same time. I wonder if he feels it, too. This…this *happiness*. This disbelief. It's like…it's like it's my first time seeing a sun rise.

I nod my assent and watch the screen sizzle before me. The female starts by saying, "Yo. This is Deena. You all won't believe this. We're on a tiny rock trading some space junk and look who I found. *Look*." The screen fades from black to clear and I realize I'm being recorded now. "Just tell them who you are, that's all. Then I'll give you two times the merillian you want. Did I say two? Make it ten!" She shouts, much to the grumbling of the pirates behind her. It makes me laugh a wet, happy laugh.

I rub my nose while heat lines my left side and then my right. I look over at my parents. My father smiles at me, wearing hides that show off the scars on his arms with pride. To my right, my mom's horns shoot up into the sky, the broken one standing as a testament to the love she has for her mate.

Behind me, Grizz loops his strong, clawed hands over my shoulders and pulls me deeper into the safety of his chest, his beast rumbling contentedly. Inhaling shakily and squeezing Grizz's hand once more, I am filled with overwhelming love as I look ahead at the female — a female who proves I do come from someplace — even if Revatu is where my soul has always belonged.

"My name is Latanya of Revatu and you don't need to worry about me. I'm loved, I'm happy and I'm safe. I'm not alone. I never have been. The stars brought me home." I smile happily.

"It's incredible, the way they do that, isn't it?" the paler of the two females says, stepping closer, a pirate at her side. She glances back at him and then at the pirates and hybrids surrounding her, before looking back at me. She blinks with just one of her eyes in an expression I find strangely conspiratorial and together, we share a proud smile.

"It is," I nod. "It's like magic."

Grizz bends down, arching over me. His warm, smoke-laced breath tickles my ear as he says, "Cera. It's like *Xiveri*."

I sincerely hope you've treasured every moment of the Xiveri Mates journey! If you loved this wacky conclusion, leave your review for Latanya and Grizz on Amazon.

From here, you can choose to dive into the other Xiveri Mates novella, Exiled from Nobu in ebook in Xiveri Mates Collection One or as a standalone in print.

Or, start from the beginning with Miari and Raku's story in Taken to Voraxia available in all formats, including audio!

Special edition and steamy NSFW Xiveri Mates editions will be made available soon, so sign up to my newsletter and be sure you don't miss out:
www.booksbyelizabeth.com/contact

Until we meet again, love like Xiveri,

Elizabeth

Exiled from Nobu

Xiveri Mates Book 2.5, a Novella (Lisbel and Jaxal)

Lisbel is a dangerous Voraxian female. Haughty and proud, she's stubborn and deserving of a punishment her human mate Jaxal is all too happy to give. But Jaxal begins to notice a slight bend to the female the longer she spends with the humans, on the colony, with him. It may just transform Lisbel into a female worth standing beside, worth slaughtering for, worth everything.

Available on Amazon in ebook as part of Xiveri Mates Collection One, or in print as a standalone

1

Lisbel

We watch each other across the space.

It's small. Filthy. Everything's covered in a thick layer of red dust. It's nothing at all like the large dome I left behind on my ice and snow-covered home, Nobu. Nox. This has nothing to do with Nobu. This little moon is covered in visible dirt, with the exception of a few black screa hills that would shred the soles of my feet right open if I dared to walk on them without shoes. Without *sandals*. That's what the humans call these flimsy foot covers.

Of course, I have more toes than they do, so I had to stuff my feet into these strappy things. My…the male who lives in this dirt house with me helped me create better straps out of reeds. Reeds. Like there is no technology. Like we aren't even within Voraxia anymore. Where are the Hogers who can make clothes custom to fit even the tallest form? Where are the Evras who can make foods for me to eat?

Where are the Xcleranx who can fight and defend me from the khrui monsters that roam ever closer to the Droherion Dome that protects this filthy human colony

— or even worse, the filthy humans *beneath* the Dome who I am supposed to be making a new life among?

In exile.

I often feel like running out of this shack that my — that *the* male calls a home and heading for those screa cliffs. I'd have better luck making a home among those wretched khrui beasts that roam this moon than I would among the humans.

How did it come to this?

The cold winds thrash and burn, but no more than usual. What burns is the knowledge that I'm on trial for crimes that I knowingly committed against the Okkari of Nobu, its ruler. I can't fight. I always wanted to learn, but my sires never allowed it. Females are too rare in Voraxia to risk allowing them into combat. Females can never be warriors. At least... that's what I believed my whole life.

My whole life, I've been wrong.

I've seen female warriors fight. Watched it with my own eyes. If such a battle hadn't ended moments ago, I'd have never believed it myself. And now I stand before warriors — male warriors and female ones — knowing that I am a criminal and knowing that I wouldn't have the strength to defend myself even if I tried.

I am humiliated. The sensation is almost enough to take me to my knees. Almost. Because there is a sensation that is miraculously stronger than this one keeping me upright. Nox. Not upright. Making me weightless. I weigh nothing against it.

I can feel a tugging in my chest, begging me to turn around. I do, and that's when I hear a groan. I don't understand the sound as I hear it, because it reverberates with tension and fear and, above all other things, lust. To call the voice male would be an injustice. It's like the universe, Xana, is speaking directly into my ear, telling me her secrets. It's like my soul, Xaneru, mate to Xana, has reached for a box inside my belly I did not know existed and unlocked it and let every emotion I didn't know I was capable of, rampage through me in the same moment.

I start to shake as I scan the crowd looking in on me, searching, searching, searching…"Fuck the sun," comes the curse in a language I can only understand because of the translation implant given to me, "I'll champion for her."

My gaze narrows on a kneeling form. As he rises, I can't believe what I see. He has dark brown skin, a shade that is not Voraxian or shared by any other species I have ever seen. His hair falls in thin ropes down his back. His eyes are just as bleak as they are black when they look up at me.

I don't understand. This is a human. And worse, this human looks at me like he despises me. He can't possibly be my… "Are you…" But I don't need to ask. I know that this human that I hate and that hates me equally is the male that the fates chose for me. He is my biological match, the one with whom procreating will be possible. Perhaps the only male with whom it can be.

He is my Xiveri Mate.

I know that he is, like I know my true name is Lisbel. Like I know the cold and the ice and the darkness that is my home. Like I know that more than anything in the world, all I have ever wanted is to be a queen and a warrior and now I never will be because my mate is a human who hates me.

"Yeah," he says, speaking like it causes him great pain. I cannot truly tell. We Voraxians wear our emotions in the colorful ridges that dot our forehead in the same place these humans have 'eyebrows.' "I'm your Ziv-whatever. Your mate. You're not fighting today, and you're not going into exile."

I didn't fight that day, but I did go into exile. I'm not sure if the human advisor called *Svera* responsible for this decision is the kindest creature I've ever met or the most sinister. Because instead of exiling me to the great white ocean where all those on Nobu are exiled — essentially, sentenced to death — she had me exiled here, to the human moon colony where I am the only alien among them and the only creature on whom I can rely is a human warrior male who thinks me disgusting even though he is bound to me for life.

"You hungry?" He says in his language, standing up from the wooden table in the center of the eating room he calls *kitch-nn*.

"Nox," I answer in my own language, ignoring the pull in my gut at the sight of his bare chest covered in a sheen of sweat because here it is always hot.

"Haven't eaten this solar."

"I don't need to eat every solar. My body is more efficient than yours. It needs less sustenance and I generate less waste." I wait for him to look at me and acknowledge the insult, but he doesn't and it annoys me more than it should.

It would be better if I could ignore him the way he ignores me. Then I could live out my sentence here in peace instead of being plagued by thoughts of him in the lunar, heat building and blossoming through me that's getting harder and harder to ignore. But from rumors I've heard, the Xanaxana affects our kind far more rapidly and more intensely than theirs. What if he only has an inkling? What if he never feels anything for me at all? *I've given him no reason to…*

"Fine. Going out." He grabs his fighting staff and a sheathed sword from the rack of weapons hanging beside our front door — *the* front door. His long hair he keeps tied back in a leather strap at the nape of his neck. The long, rope-like tips swish against his lower back where there are two subtle indents. I lick my lips. He isn't my kind — he isn't even a ruler among his — but I do seem to like the shape of him.

"Where?" I say as he opens the front door and the miserable sight of this red planet greets me.

I already know the answer. "Training field."

"So you can attempt to redeem yourself after failing on Nobu's ice flats?" It's a low insult, one I've made before.

And it never works. "No. Don't see myself fighting in the snow anytime soon."

He steps through the door.

"Wait."

He waits.

"What should I do?"

"Don't know. Don't care." He doesn't look back at me.

"I won't be here when you return."

"So you've said the past seventeen solars." Seventeen solars. That's how long I've been on this Xana-forsaken rock. That's how many vows I've made to run. That's how many times I've reneged on that suicidal vow.

"Well, I'm not staying here."

He chuffs, looking at me and his eyes are dark and his face is so well formed. *Perhaps, even more well-formed than the Okkari's.* I wince at the thought of how I debased myself with him, of the lies I told the Xhea of Nobu so that I might usurp her place, little knowing that my attempt would bring my own Xiveri Mate onto Nobu's shores. He is a *friend* of hers. I'm not familiar with this concept and I hate the term. It means other females can approach my Xiveri and speak with him, share their true names with him because these humans don't even use titles. And, if his affection for me is so little, perhaps even *lay* with him while I sit here pining after a male I loathe.

"Never told you you had to. In fact, you shouldn't be here. You should be out there gettin' to work. There's lotsa shit to do, helpin' with the construction of the birthing center, or building the new houses."

"I don't build."

"Food's gotta get made. Cooks could always use a hand."

"I don't cook."

He looks at me, long and lingering. "Then do whatever you want."

"I want to leave."

"Not stoppin' you."

"You're hardly a warrior — you can't."

He grins with one side of his mouth and it transforms his face. Utterly spellbinding. "Against a fierce warrior like you? Wouldn't dream of tryin', princess." His wink and his stupid, cavalier grin only serves to make the insult more cutting before he disappears, shutting the door in his wake.

Continue reading in print as a standalone or in ebook as part of Xiveri Mates Collection One

What to read next

Lord of Population (Population Book 1)
When Abel comes across one of the alien overlords, she loots his corpse, the good little scavenger she is. She doesn't expect his death to be erm, temporary. He hunts her down and gives her a choice. Accept his help... The catch? She's now his.

This is a sci-fi, fantasy, post-apocalyptic romance mashup with a guaranteed HEA and plenty of slow burn steam. Tropes include enemies-to-reluctant allies-to-lovers, found family, he falls first, he rescues her, she rescues him, she has a nightmare, "who did this to you", one bed

The Hunting Town (Twisted Fates Book 1)
Drugs, cartels, the mafia. Pain, greed, and revenge. These are what Plumeria brought with her when she took a new job tending bar in the fighting pits outside of town – fighting pits owned by five men, known as the Brothers. Knox wouldn't have put anything before his brothers – not even his own life – until he met Mer. But when her life is put at risk, he intervenes, dragging his entire family into her world.

This is a romantic suspense featuring two couples that both reach their HEA. The first couple are two cage fighters, the second a medical student turned exotic dancer and the grump who owns the club. Plenty of steam and mayhem await.

Dark City Omega (Berserker Kings Book 1)
There are three absolutes for any Omega who has the misfortune of finding herself in Paradise Hole:

The first - stay away from the cities.
The second - stay off the road.
The third - stay away from Alphas.

Echo knew the rules. She just never expected to be hunted by a lord among Alphas, by a Berserker himself, the savage of Dark City. But he's been on her scent for six weeks.

And now, he's found her.

Coming soon, this is an action-packed dark fantasy romance ripe with spice, magic, and battles and perfect for fans of diverse books, possessive heroes and strong lady leads. Tropes include omegaverse, enemies-to reluctant allies-to lovers, fated mates-ish, one sleeping mat, trek through the forest together, she's injured, he saves her, she saves him, grumpxgrump

All Books by Elizabeth

Berserker Kings - Enemies to lovers. With magic.
Dark City Omega, Book 1 (Echo and Adam)
more to come!

Population - Battles and Heroes that Bite.
Lord of Population, Book 1 (Abel and Kane)
Monster in the Oasis, Book 2 (Diego and Pia)
Immortal with Scars, Book 3 (Lahve and Candy)
more to come!

Twisted Fates - Mafia. Brotherhood. Murder.
The Hunting Town, Book 1 (Knox and Mer, Dixon and Sara)
The Hunted Rise, Book 2 (Aiden and Alina, Gavriil and Ify)
The Hunt, Book 3 (Anatoly and Candy, Charlie and Molly)

Xiveri Mates - Aliens. Heat. New Worlds.
Taken to Voraxia, Book 1 (Miari and Raku)
Taken to Nobu, Book 2 (Kiki and Va'Raku)
Exiled from Nobu, Book 2.5, a Novella (Lisbel and Jaxal)
Taken to Sasor, Book 3 (Mian and Neheyuu) *standalone
Taken to Heimo, Book 4 (Svera and Krisxox)
Taken to Kor, Book 5 (Deena and Rhork)
Taken to Lemora, Book 6 (Essmira and Raingar)
Taken by the Pikosa Warlord, Book 7 (Halima and Ero)
*standalone
Taken to Evernor, Book 8 (Nalia and Herannathon)
Taken to Sky, Book 9 (Ashmara and Jerrock)
Taken to Revatu, Book 10, A Novella (Latanya and Grizz)
*standalone

Collections

Xiveri Mates - Aliens. Heat. New Worlds.
Collection 1: Books 1-3 + Exiled from Nobu
More to come!

Audiobooks

Xiveri Mates - Aliens. Heat. New Worlds.
Taken to Voraxia, Book 1 (Miari and Raku)
Taken to Nobu, Book 2 (Kiki and Va'Raku)
Taken to Sasor, Book 3 (Mian and Neheyuu) *standalone
More to come!

French Language

**Passion Xiveri : Unis Pour La Vie – Des extraterrestres.
De la sensualité. De nouveaux mondes.**
Capturée par le Roi de Voraxia, tome 1 (Miari et Raku)
Convoitée par le Seigneur de guerre de Nobu, tome 2
(Kiki et Va'Raku)
Kidnappée par le Métamorphe de Sasor, tome 3 (Mian et
Neheyuu) *l'intrigue se situe hors du Quadrant 4
D'autres livres seront bientôt publiés !